Gulabiya

Praise for the Book

'What good fortune for readers that skilled translators Shivangi and Tejaswi have brought this Angika gem into English! *Gulabiya* is a short, punchy read from the rural heartland that gives us a gutsy new heroine to love.'

– Daisy Rockwell, International Booker Prize–winning translator

'A rare translation from Angika, *Gulabiya* is a masterfully crafted novella whose succinct style and economy of words draw the reader in from the very beginning. From the inner lives of the farmhands and other villagers to a commentary on caste and class struggle, Dr Abha Purbey tackles everything with an adept pen. The translation shows a command of the craft, with the emotions of the characters in this working-class love story jumping right off the pages.'

– Vaibhav Sharma, literary translator

'Abha Purbey's novel squarely confronts the impact of caste politics on individual lives and choices in India. It is written in Angika, a language used only in some parts of the state of Bihar and Jharkhand, which is apt, since its characters live this language. Shivangi and Tejaswi fiercely guard the unique rhythms and use of words in the translation of a work that challenges both linguistic and social stereotypes.'

– Jury, Armory Square Prize for South Asian Literature in Translation

Gulabiya

A NOVEL

DR ABHA PURBEY

Translated from the Angika by

Tejaswi Rawal • Shivangi

hachette INDIA

First published in Angika in 2008 by Angika Sansad, Bhagalpur
This translation first published in 2026 by Hachette India
(Registered name: Hachette Book Publishing India Pvt. Ltd)
An Hachette UK company
www.hachetteindia.com

1

Subsequent edition/reprint specifications may be subject to change, including but not limited to cover or inside finishes, paper, text colour, and/or colour sections.

Print ISBN 978-93-5731-932-4
eBook ISBN 978-93-5731-454-1

Hachette Book Publishing India Pvt. Ltd
4th & 5th Floors, Corporate Centre,
Plot No. 94, Sector 44, Gurugram 122003, India

Typeset in Dante MT Std 12/16
by R. Ajith Kumar, New Delhi

Printed and bound in India
by Manipal Technologies Limited

MIX
Paper | Supporting responsible forestry
FSC www.fsc.org FSC™ C043100

Contents

1

Summer is here, and it is brutal. But not yet so bad that a few minutes in the sun will scorch you. Labourers are hard at work, their bodies weary from the heat. Near the farmhands, Gulabiya is digging. Whether or not the shovel makes its way through the earth doesn't seem to concern her.

Gulabiya is in the fields, but her mind is elsewhere; Balesar is not here yet. He knows that she's waiting for him. He has to come today. *Yesterday, he had promised that he would definitely come see me today*. As the sun gathers its rays, a worry rises in her heart. Her hands go numb, as if no strength remains in them. Shivers run through her body.

Gulabiya's heart isn't in the work. With every passing minute, the question tugs at her: why isn't Balesar here yet? Did his boss keep him back on purpose, giving him more work? Could it be that he has found out about the love blossoming between her and Balesar? Come to think of it, Patel Singh, the boss, was monitoring her very closely that day. She didn't understand why. It's possible that one of the labourers has said something. Men and snakes are kindred spirits. They can switch loyalties any minute. They'll be sweet to your face but gossip behind your back.

All this worrying is futile. But until Balesar himself arrives and explains, she can think of nothing else. Balesar has never been this late. He always arrives when he says he will, usually with time to spare. His tardiness today fills her with a strange kind of despair. She isn't spending time, she's bleeding time. She makes up her mind: while he isn't here, she'll keep working, even if it means working late into the night. If she goes home today, it will be with Balesar, and for that, she will wait as long as it takes.

Some of the workers start packing up their things, preparing to leave. Gulabiya is so deep in her thoughts that she doesn't register what's happening around her – who's looking at her, who's talking about her. Nothing. But her closest friend, Paro, takes notice. She sees the perverse curiosity on the labourers' faces and admonishes them.

'Why are you people staring at Gulabiya? She comes to work every day. You see her every day. Why stare at her like this? Is there something new today? Go, go home. Go to the market.' Her temper rises as she speaks.

When has a man ever silently accepted a woman's anger? The only men who stay silent in response are either scared of women or don't care about them. A few of the workers who aren't particularly interested in the unfolding scene pick up their bags and leave, but Somen, who knows Gulabiya well, glares at Paro with his large, round eyes, stroking his moustache.

'Why? Do we not have the right to use our god-given eyes to see? We didn't say anything unseemly to her. We just looked with our eyes. Why are you so bothered? It's a man's job to feast his eyes on a woman. We work together. How long are we supposed to just shut our eyes? And then, your friend is so beautiful. It's hard to look at anything else when she's around. It's not like Gulabiya is a grand thakurain that a common man daren't meet her gaze.' After saying this, had he not got up and left quietly, Paro would have given him an earful, the kind he'd never heard, not even from his masters.

But what can she do? What will she get out of fighting these workers? She and Gulabo will have to come back to these very fields to work.

She is angry with Gulabiya now. What has happened to this girl? She looks at her, sitting there with a shovel in her hand. So lost in thought that she doesn't realize that her saree is beginning to slip off. Her hair is dishevelled from working. Seeing her in this state deflates Paro.

She thinks of what Somen said: 'Your friend is really beautiful. She'd catch anyone's eye.' Her gaze falls on Gulabiya, like a chakor looks at the moon. But would the chakor have looked at the moon if it had seen Gulabiya first? Paro looks at her intently. Gulabiya does look especially beautiful today, truly striking, in her pink saree and blue blouse. It seems she came to work dressed up to meet someone.

But Gulabiya is beautiful even when she doesn't dress up. Honestly, she is the very picture of beauty. Fair as a dove, a full, round face on a full body. Big eyes and a proud, prominent nose. *If I am so taken by this beauty, then is it really surprising if a man is beside himself for her?*

But underneath the admiration, Paro is still seething. *What has happened to this girl? Her head is in the clouds, completely unaware of herself, not a worry in the world. God knows if she's going home or not. None of her things are in order yet. She can't be left here by herself. Not in this state.* Paro shakes her violently to bring her back to her senses.

'Ae, Gulabiya, Gulabo, Gulabo' – but Gulabiya doesn't respond. It isn't that she is unconscious. She is wide awake, and yet she isn't. Paro shakes her once again. 'Gulabo!'

Gulabiya's body is still. As motionless as a stone idol.

Paro holds Gulabiya's face in her hands and makes their gazes meet. 'Gulabo, Gulabo, look, the evening is upon us. You and I are the only people left in this field. Come home with me, Gulabo. What is this love rubbish you're caught up in? You've ruined your health for love. Everyone knows how to fall in love, you know, and yet, only a few know how to fulfil love's duties. Even fewer amongst men.'

Gulabiya is still. Her face has a glimmer of hope. She only speaks when Paro shakes her relentlessly. She takes Paro's hands in her own and says, 'Balesar will come. He really loves me.'

Paro doesn't believe this at all. Her heart refuses to believe it after seeing her friend's state. But who will tell Gulabo? Paro begs her to understand. 'Gulabo, what is this sickness you've brought upon yourself?'

Tears well up in Gulabiya's eyes. Holding onto Paro's hands, she says, 'You won't understand, Paro. I've chosen a lifelong sickness by falling in love. Do you know Radha? The one who loved Krishna? For a bit of love, she devoted her life to him. Little did she know her love would take this shape. Today, there's but one name on every lover's lips. 'Radhe–Krishna… Radhe–Krishna… '

'Gulabo, forget all this love nonsense and let's go home. Even the rays of the sun have hidden their faces.' Paro tries to pull her up by the arm.

But Gulabiya seems to have sunk further into the ground. Freeing her hand from Paro's grip, she says, 'Paro, my Balesar means as much to me as Krishna meant to Meera. Like an idol, he is always in front of my eyes. Where will I go if I leave him here? Meera's Krishna was made of stone. My Balesar is a living, breathing human being. Can you imagine how heartbroken he'll be without me?' She goes back to staring in the direction of the road that Balesar takes daily.

Gulabiya's crazy behaviour makes Paro angrier. She tugs at Gulabiya's hand harder, making her stand up. Still full of an anger that can only be born out of love, she begs, 'Gulabo, will you come home or not? I will not listen to this love nonsense anymore. It's evening now. It's time to go light the lamps at home. My mother is waiting for me. Swear on my life that you'll listen to me just this once.'

Gulabiya's heart is still heavy. She doesn't want to leave. Paro knows this very well, but she isn't going to stay here any longer, and neither is she going to let Gulabo stay – not on this farm that increasingly reminds her of a dark, menacing forest. Her grip on Gulabo tightens, and she hardens her heart.

Gulabo continues to sink into the earth like Shiva. No, no! No matter what happens, even if Gulabo actually transforms into a Shiva idol affixed to the ground, Paro is not going to let her stay here. She grabs her and pulls. Suddenly, as if by magic, Gulabo's body, which a moment ago felt as heavy as a stone, becomes light as a feather. Paro takes her in her arms and leaves the field; two shadows walking in the dusk. It almost seems as if Balesar is carrying Gulabiya in his arms. Taking her far, far away.

2

For the fourth day in a row, Seth Patel Singh had kept Balesar working until four. Even the traces of a smile had left his face. He'd gone quiet and didn't want to be at the farm anymore. He stood there alone, staring into the distance.

He hadn't reprimanded the workers even once. Usually, they'd get an earful even if they were hard at work. The workers took advantage of Balesar's inattention. They did as little as possible and tried to leave early. A couple of them at first, but soon everyone wanted to go home. Normally, it would be 4.30 p.m. before Balesar let them go.

Something had changed in Balesar when he emerged as the leader of the farmhands and the landowner appointed him manager, making him responsible for squeezing work out of them. Balesar was a domineering boss. He knew how to get them to work. Nobody lazed around for long under his watch. Then, one day, things came back around. Patel Singh began to hand him a list of chores at the crack of dawn. It was his turn to be put under pressure.

He wanted to check off everything on the list as soon as possible and steal a moment to see Gulabiya – to apologize and make up. But he hadn't made a dent in the workload. Whenever a worker asked permission to leave, he'd wordlessly gesture his assent. Chamru, a farmhand, observed this from a distance with great interest. Chamru was a large man with an inky complexion and a thick upper lip that sat a bit too high on his face, his mouth resembling a tiger's snout. His nose wasn't very prominent, but it was hypermobile, constantly going up and down his face.

Chamru's nose twitched. He brought his hands to his sides, took out the comb tucked into his lungi, and continued to monitor Balesar closely. Balesar was completely unaware of this. Chamru raised his hand, holding the comb up to the sky, and then, with a stylish flick of the wrist, brought it downward and ran it through his hair.

Chamru had always been bold. Whenever he felt like leaving, he just walked by Balesar, combing his hair, and Balesar never said a word. Today, rather than strolling out, he decided to go to Balesar and conduct an enquiry first. 'Balesar, why the long face? Did something happen at home?' His voice dripped with sarcasm.

The few workers who hadn't yet left turned to look at Balesar – he did seem sad. But why?

Nobody comprehended the storm raging within him.

Balesar didn't respond except to say, 'You guys go collect your wages from the maalik.' He then set off for home.

A few people tried to talk to him on the way, but he didn't look back. One of them was Sohan Kaka, a distant relative of his who also worked on the farm. Usually, Balesar would be thrilled to see him. He'd tease Kaka, 'Looks like there was an extra helping of love in the fish today, eh, Kaka? Your face is glowing from within,' and Kaka would feign anger, then burst out laughing. But he did not tease Kaka today. He didn't even turn around when Kaka called out his name.

Kaka was worried about Balesar. Why did he not talk to him? Why did he not tease him?

According to village tradition, Balesar's relationship with Kaka's wife was that of nephew and aunt, but she was close to him in age, and they weren't bound by formality. He'd often grab her by the wrist and taunt her about how he'd caught Kaka in the theatre the night before. Today, when she tried to grab his arm, he shook her off and walked ahead. He didn't want people to look at him.

Balesar got to his house and lay down on the mat; rather, he threw himself to the ground and landed with a wham. It was a part of his routine to light a diya or an incense stick as soon as he got home, but not today. Today, when he looked at the incense, he was reminded of the day a few months ago when he'd fought with Singh for keeping him late at the farms, keeping him from seeing Gulabo...

He didn't like having to work long after the other labourers had gone home, but Singh always found some excuse to keep him back. So that day, he had just got up and left. He'd decided that he wasn't going to work for him anymore. The other labourers tried to reason with him, saying that he was being unreasonable and foolish – *What will you do if not this? If the boss fires us, what will we do?* It had fallen on deaf ears. Balesar knew that having two hands was enough for a working man in this world.

He quit the farm and decided to sit at home for a few days, but the very next day, the maalik came, imploring him to return. He said, 'You know that you're the most honest and hardworking labourer I have. You also know that all my farms depend on you. *You* manage the farms from now on. You look after them.' From then on, he was the manager.

He wouldn't have accepted that position if it weren't for the fact that quitting the farm meant he wouldn't see Gulabiya as often. Nobody understood what happened to him when he couldn't see her. This was something only they knew – him and Gulabiya, his Gulabo.

That day, Gulabo wafted, dreamlike, through the shabby wooden door of his hut. *Is this real?* If Gulabiya hadn't covered his eyes with her hands, he would have continued to look at her for an eternity.

She broke the silence. 'I hear you're a manager now? Is this how the high and mighty live? The sheets are on the clothesline, and Manager Babu is on a straw mat on the floor. The stink from the next alley fills your room, and the incense sticks lie in a corner.' She continued to ramble on as she lit an incense stick and put it in a recess in the wall. 'I came with Poobari Chachi. She went to meet Kamli Mai, and I snuck out. I'm going to leave now.' And then, as if whisked away by the wind, she was gone.

Like a dream, this memory played in his head on a loop.

He blinked. It was dawn.

He hadn't slept all night. Thanks to Singh's constant bullying, he felt less like a manager and more like a bonded labourer. He decided he wasn't going to be bound anymore.

Colour returned to his cheeks as he made this decision. It was as if a weight had lifted from his head. For days, he'd been carrying a mountain around. Just like that, it was gone. Now, his head felt light as a feather. The house that had been closing in on him for a week now smelled of jasmine, no... no... it smelled of roses. In this room that smelled of roses, he thought of his rose – Gulabo. He spread his hands across the sheets as if she were sitting there. *She made this bed. This is such a wonderful bed.* He didn't just run his fingers over the sheets; he traced them across Gulabiya's hands – the same hands that had made this bed.

Outside, the birds grew louder. Balesar wrapped the sheets around himself. He didn't want them to get dirty – and why wouldn't they? All day, the wind came from Kosi carrying the sand and the dirt, dumping them straight into the house. In a few hours, this entire house would become Kosi Ma's bed. He started to hum as he got up.

Das Kabir jatan se odhi, jas ke tas dhar dini chadaria. He wore it with great care and put it back as it was.

He wasn't going to let the sheets get dirty. Was his love even true if he did? He hung them on the clothesline, but that didn't feel right. Then he tried the hook on the wall where his shirt hung. He put on the shirt and hung the sheets. Finally, he left the house, the birds, and the wind behind, and went towards Kosi.

He carefully opened the bamboo gate in front of his house. The feeling rose in his heart that he should visit the river Kosi before sunrise. Ever since becoming Seth Patel Singh's manager, his life had been so limited. He looked at the birds, now visible in the faint sunlight, flying in the sky, and thought that he, too, was like a bird – free. There was nothing like freedom. Freedom from all bondage. A golden prison with great food is still a prison. It sits on your heart like a weight. A bird likes to fly, and she eats whatever she finds. Everyone likes to be free...

From now on, I, too, like a bird, am free.

For the past few months, he had been a captive bird. He had had every luxury, and labourers had trembled before him. And yet, his so-called freedom was a prison. For so long, he hadn't even had the time to go down to the river.

First, he went to Patel Singh's field and cleaned his teeth with a date stick. After so long, he would scrub his back with bamboo. He looked around, a bamboo cane in his hand. Truly, everything looked wonderful today. The spring sky was open and clear. Even it was without worry. As if it had nowhere to rush. A smile flitted across Balesar's face.

Ganga snan kare le chali gagal hai niya, Ganga Mai. We are off for a dip in the Ganga, O Ganga Ma!

Someone was walking by singing this song. Balesar listened closely. He'd heard these songs from childhood and always thought them lovely. He hummed as he walked along. Not songs of the Ganges; songs Gulabiya's heart lived in.

Still humming, he walked towards the eastern riverbank. Seeing him, the group of women stepped out of his path. Balesar didn't know where to sit. Nanaki Bhouji couldn't resist teasing him. She bit her lip and, smiling, said, 'Well, Balesar Deor, you've finally found the time to come down here? Ever since you've become the manager, it's as if you've forgotten your sister-in-law. The brother-in-law may forget, but his sister-in-law can never forget him. We all think of you every day. You never have any time for us.'

Balesar responded to Nanaki Bhouji's teasing in kind. 'Bhouji, I was desperate to meet you all. Bathing in the

Ganga with all of you as my companions is a pleasure like no other. There's no laughing and joking on the fields. Being Patel Singh's manager means I miss out on everything. Come now, let's tie the knot and bathe in the Ganga together!'

His wit had met its match in Nanaki. Every bit as teasing, she said, 'I have no problem with tying the knot with you. The problems will begin when Gulabo hauls me over the coals!' The group of women tittered. The tune of this song had changed; Balesar was struck speechless.

How? How did Nanaki Bhouji know his innermost feelings? He felt as if a raincloud had burst over his head. But just as quickly, he got a hold of himself. Maybe Nanaki Bhouji had thought nothing of it, and was just joking in her light-hearted, mischievous way. *And it was me, the part of my mind keeping a secret and sneaking about, that suddenly felt exposed. And even if she does know, that's alright. In fact, better if people have an inkling, rather than having it suddenly revealed.* The smile was restored to his face. He glanced at the women once more, and then set off in the direction of Patel Singh's farm.

When he arrived at the fields, not a single worker was in sight. It was surprising that on this day, even though he'd taken the time to bathe, and made his way swaying and swinging, unhurriedly, he'd managed to arrive at dawn. Ordinarily, he'd hurry here, and the labourers would already be there. Could this be an illusion of his mind? It was certainly true that he had arrived at the field at daybreak – almost as if he'd done everything in a hurry since he'd woken up, though he knew he had gone about the start of his day at a leisurely pace. Perhaps, because he had no work at the field today, everything just seemed out of place.

See, now, the labourers are slowly arriving.

The workers were confused to see Balesar sitting idly in the field, when he had the day off.

Some workers were there just after dawn, while the others were late. They thought that Balesar must have come down to keep an eye on them, to see who was doing what: who was arriving late, and who had been there at sunrise. They all spontaneously approached Balesar where he sat, giving their reasons for being late. Balesar listened with an intent expression, all the while smiling internally. He didn't reprimand anyone or say anything. Having delivered their excuses, everyone set about their work for the day. The fear that had gripped them not long ago was gone, and they'd returned to their loose and lackadaisical ways. Today, Balesar didn't deliver any admonishments.

Ever since he'd become the manager, he'd taken out a lot of anger and frustration on the labourers. Chamru, Mangru, Basanta, Mandar, Sitbiya and all the others were doing their own work. Well, not quite – they were passing the time till they could go home. Today, Balesar didn't care about this at all. He watched them working at their own pace, and thought silently, *Like me, they are all workers. Why should I rebuke them, shout at them?* Watching Mangru work at a fast pace, he jumped up and, drawing close to him, held his hand still. Taking Mangru's hoe, he said, 'What, Mangru, what's the rush? It'll get done. What will you get by rushing? Yes, if the owner paid more for more work, that'd be one thing. You might work your body to exhaustion for more money. But extra work has no value here. Even if you toil all day, you'll make the same amount of money. So don't work so hard. Protect your body. It's only through this body that you have anything in this world, and only as long as you're able-bodied will owners and landlords ask after you. This is what the elders say, and it is the greatest truth in the world.'

Balesar let them get on with it at their pace. He did not want them to work too hard. The workers were shocked to see this side of Balesar. What had happened to him? Usually, he would show anger, and now he was suddenly being loving and caring. But no one said a word. Chamru raised his eyes and looked up at Balesar, trying to read his face, but he couldn't guess his inner feelings. Today, Balesar wasn't lording his managerial status over anyone.

It seemed to take forever for dawn to break and the sun to bring the day. As Balesar watched, the sun god climbed higher, and soon his forehead felt the rays of light. The workers took out their food and prepared to eat. Balesar, though, kept standing to the side. When he had been just a labourer, like Chamru, he would eat with everyone else. He would open the bag of chura or sattu he had brought with him. But for a while, Balesar had been eating and drinking at a remove from the labourers. Today, he did not move away, though he hadn't brought anything to eat.

What might the workers have been thinking as he hovered over them? They sat on the ground in a group, not opening their parcels of food, when Balesar said to Chamru, 'What, Chamru da, won't you sit and eat with me today?' Balesar quickly sat down amongst them. He opened Chamru's parcel, tossing a bit of chura ka bhunja into his mouth, and said, 'Everyone, take out your food. Let's all eat together.' Mangru, Basanta, Chamru, Mandar, Sitbiya – everyone brought out their sattu and added their salt and spices.

Balesar piped up again. 'Today I will sit amongst you all and eat. It's been a long time since I sat down to eat and drink with you.' He paused, chewing on Chamru's chura, and continued, 'I'm the same species of bird as you, Mangru, aren't I? Think for yourself, how cunningly Maalik Patel Singh, the hunter, has separated me from you. I was another bird amongst birds. He turned me into a falcon to attack you. What I mean is, he made us divide ourselves into separate species. Now Patel Singh is only happy with me if I suck all the blood and sweat out of people for him, the hunter.'

Chamru listened intently, his eyes burrowing into Balesar. Balesar wanted to tell them what was on his mind, to feel lighter. For so long, he'd carried a burden. This felt good. Enthusiasm rose in his chest. Making him a manager had really been a punishment from Patel Singh. He had caused a rift between Balesar and the others, broken their bonds.

Chamru felt happy to hear Balesar express this. Before Balesar could finish talking, Mangru began to tell them of an experience from his past.

Mangru had a wheatish complexion and a wide chest. Atop his broad, proud forehead flourished a head of thick black hair. His wide nose sat above ever-smiling lips. He always wore a certain pride that he'd worked in

Calcutta city. Had luck been with him, he wouldn't have worked as a wage labourer. He knew what their status was. *If they wanted to, they could do great things without any education, these illiterate and ignorant people. One just needed to have a plan in mind.*

Mangru took out some khaini and pushed it into his gums, under his thick lower lip. 'You're right, Balesar. You know that I worked in Calcutta for ten years. But you don't know the way the communists rule there. We had ministers who advocated for the workers. One evening, when we returned to our room, an older comrade heard us talking amongst ourselves. He then told us a story, which has suddenly come back to me, Balesar, after hearing what you've said. This story is not from our country, you know. This is a tale from a distant land. He said that across the seven seas there is a land. He told us its name. Ah, see, I've forgotten…' Mangru tried to recall the name of this faraway place, pressing his hand against his forehead. After a while, he said, 'What can I tell you? This khaini crushes all my intelligence.' He shook his head, then suddenly it came to him. 'Yes, I remember! That country is called Rome. There, they would buy men, the way we buy sheep and goats.

'Kings would buy men and enslave them. Bought men were the measure of a king's strength and wealth. What kind of life did a man have, sold like a cucumber in the market, and cut up and killed according to the whims of whoever bought him?'

Basanta, eager to hear the rest of Mangru's story, his hands clasped in his lap, didn't even realize that he had stopped eating, waiting for Mangru to go on. Sitbiya, who had been sitting a little farther away, had moved closer. His curiosity had so captured him that he didn't notice the food stuck between his teeth; he had stopped chewing at some point. Mangru's silence only fed their curiosity further. Mandar watched his face closely, waiting for him to continue, then finally asked, 'What next?'

'Those who live a life where they can't do anything through their own will always have a fire smouldering within them. But no slave can speak up. Well, also, the slaves there received many benefits from their masters. Think of Balesar, for example. Patel Singh made him a manager and gave him some advantages. He feeds him, and if he needs something, he quickly provides. Look how Balesar was treated better than us as soon as he became the manager. It's incredibly rare for any of us to go to Patel Singh's house, but Balesar can come and go as he pleases.'

As Mangru narrated, a glint appeared in his eyes. 'But despite having so many luxuries, one thing remained difficult: he could never speak his mind, he could never do as he pleased. What the owner wants, the slave must do. Slaves in Rome were fed the best food to keep their bodies strong and able. They were made to exercise. They were even given teachers.'

Chamru, always a smart aleck, didn't believe Mangru. He asked if all the king did was feed and educate his slaves. Mangru bristled, then continued, 'No, Chamru. When the slaves were ready, they were forced to fight each other. An arena was set up specially for people to watch the fight. Kings and nobles travelled from afar to watch. In fact, the king would pay the slaves' masters to watch them fight. The slaves were skilled knife-fighters, with small blades as their weapons. Some slaves from Africa were experts at using fishing nets and tridents as weapons. Crowds of spectators from both Africa and Rome would assemble. Slaves who won popular battles were allowed some freedom for a short while.

'But how long could this last? How long can you live with having to kill your brothers? There comes a time when you can no longer continue to live like that.

'There was one slave named Spartacus. When he was taken down to the arena, watching other slaves die in these show battles filled him with a thirst for revenge. These were people like him, forced to die. A fire raged within him.' Mangru's face turned red as he described the heat of Spartacus's feeling. His breath was ragged. Patel Singh had enslaved them. In this kind of slavery, the master enjoys many pleasures, but the slave bleeds and dies.

Composing himself, he carried on. 'Chamru, do you know what Spartacus did?'

In astonishment, Chamru replied, 'What did he do, Mangru?'

Mangru suppressed the tide that rose in his mind. There was something he wanted to say, but he was no Spartacus. 'It took him a lot of thinking to make up his mind to do this. Where slaves were brutally and cruelly slaughtered, their bodies were also hung in the arena. This was meant to break their spirits. But it had the opposite effect on Spartacus. If he was destined to die, why not let out the fire burning within him before he was gone? As soon as Spartacus was brought into the fray, he attacked his master.' So ended Mangru's story, but his audience could not process that it had come to a close. They had been thrown into a state of astonishment and continued to stare at him as if waiting for more. The group looked like they'd gathered in the chaupal to chat, not come to the fields to work.

Mangru turned to Balesar. 'This story was about workers like us. What do you think?'

Balesar, lost somewhere in a world of his own, started and said, 'Did you say something, Mangru?'

Mangru was surprised to see a strange smile on Balesar's face. Though Balesar seemed not to have heard a word of Mangru's story, he answered anyway, 'Yes, Mangru. You're completely right. After all, who wants to be a slave? I don't. I won't work in Patel Singh's field anymore. I will farm on my own now. I'm going to take a loan and farm. You are right, Mangru.'

'Nowadays, you can get loans for farming and small things too,' Mangru responded. 'Panchayat mukhiyas give loans, banks give loans, there's the Farmer Income Plan, NRPE gives loans and helps the poor. All the worker needs is his resolve. And Balesar, you know, don't you, that you can ask for a loan from the BDO at the block?'

After listening to all this, Balesar had made up his mind. Somehow, he'd take a loan from somewhere to start farming on his own. There was joy in tilling your own soil.

Once Balesar had decided, it was final. From today onwards, he would not work in these fields. Without saying another word, he got up and left. Nothing could tie him to the field anymore. Not the trees, not the shrubs, not the pond, nor the fresh water from the boreholes.

Until a few days ago, these things had been dear to him, but now, deserting them, he felt nothing.

He left everything, forgot it all, as if he was turning away from a cremation, ready to move forward. Onward.

3

The month of Chait-Baishakh was underway. The heat had arrived. Mornings this time of year are pleasant, as a coolness lingers, but as the day rolls in, the cool air disperses like the vapour of camphor. Gradually, the sun makes its presence felt. As the sun god rises, the body and hands heat up. What a strange month is the month of Chait-Baishakh. Neither can the body be cool nor the mind be calm. As the influence of the sun increases, so does the anxiety of the mind. One imagines extinguishing this heat by burrowing into the earth to avoid the sun, or spending all day submerged in cold streams and ponds. But where can you do this? Where is the time for it? How will one eat without work? You have to do the work.

Balesar, knowing all this, started working.

Balesar had started running around, looking for a loan. He had to walk eight kilometres to the block, but he had a belief that no matter what, he would get the loan, so he did not care about the sun or the wind. Journeying in the heat, he was soon soaked in sweat. Not a single corner of his kurta was spared. It was so sunny that sitting in a banana field offered no respite from the intense heat.

Out in the banana field, the sun and the wind enveloped Balesar's body, mingling with the heat of his breath. The sunshine of Baishakh is something else, and on top of that, he was sitting in Kosi Ma's lap, her humidity soaking him. He had set out, and he would keep going, but he couldn't contemplate how he'd deal with meeting the sun again on his way back. Now, the great Balesar was lying flat on his face, sunlight dripping down his eyelids, as he slowly opened and shut them, half-conscious. When the sun shone into the corners of his eyes, they burned as if someone had rubbed chilli into them. He took the gamcha on his shoulder and wiped his face, remembering that Gulabiya had used this very piece of cloth to wipe her hands. Wiping his face with this handkerchief felt as if Gulabiya was wiping away the heat of the sun from him with her soft hands. The thought gave him great comfort.

For a moment, he felt as if the sun had suddenly become soft. Completely soft. The memory of Gulabiya had a wonderful effect on him. But after all, the sun is the sun. And that day's sun could boil away any tender feelings. Balesar felt like an earthen pot on the hearth. He unbuttoned his sweaty shirt and blew air down his chest in an effort to cool himself down.

Walking on, Balesar finally reached the block, but by the time he arrived, he was crushed to pieces with exhaustion.

Balesar wiped himself again and sat down outside the office. He couldn't find peace even in the shade. He took off his shirt and squeezed out the sweat, as if it were a sodden handkerchief. Then he laid it across his body and closed his eyes, trying to think of ice and coolness. He tried to control his breathing. His thoughts raced as he sat on the office stairs.

Men were coming and going from the office – a swell of people at the door. Balesar, too, got up to go in. Inside, he saw a fat man sitting at a table. He seemed to be a big man, with the others all standing or sitting around him. Dutta Babu had told him that if he saw a fat man surrounded by a crowd, that would be the man in charge. Balesar carried with him an application letter he had asked Dutta Babu to write. He'd wrapped this carefully in a plastic bag to keep it from harm. He took the papers out and flattened them, then decided to make sure he wasn't mistaken about the man by asking another person in the office.

The other man's tone was even and disengaged as he gave Balesar all the facts – 'Yes, that fat guy, the Bada Babu, is the one in charge. His name is Sumer Singh; he just arrived ten days ago.'

Balesar looked around and saw a couple of men sitting in pants and kurtas and sipping tea. Then, he looked closely at Bada Babu.

It occurred to him then that he'd seen this man before – six or seven days ago, with Patel Singh. Patel Singh–Sumer Singh. Could it be that they were related? Balesar's thoughts flew about, entering various windows of possibility. He had to get this done. If he gave his name and address, Bade Babu could help him. But if Bade Babu Sumer Singh told Patel Singh, he might not get a loan. Patel Singh wouldn't want him to have an acre or two of his own for banana farming. *But then again, why would Sumer Singh tell Patel Singh? The work here is to help the poor. Why shouldn't he help me? Actually, maybe saying Patel Singh's name will make him pay attention*. Balesar stepped forward to hand over his application.

Sumer Singh was busy talking to another man. He took the application letter and placed it under a file on his desk. Balesar was happy to see that Sumer Singh had taken his letter; surely, he would be able to do something for him. Not looking at Balesar, Sumer Singh gestured for him to sit down and wait. Full of hope and expectation, Balesar sat right outside the office. He watched several people come and go. He thought they all must be trying to get loans too.

After a while, Balesar was called back in. He felt happy. He'd get a loan now. Sumer Singh sat there on his chair. Balesar went in front of him and stood with folded hands. Still sitting casually, Sumer Singh asked, 'What is your name?'

Hesitantly, with his hands still folded in front of him, came his reply, 'Balesar.'

'What is your father's name?'

'Shivcharan.'

'Shivcharan what?'

'Shivcharan Mandal.'

'So say that then. With just Shivcharan, what god will understand anything? What work do you do?'

'I do farming.'

'What do you want?'

'Loan.'

'For what?'

'For farming.'

'A loan for farming.' Bade Babu's eyes widened to the size of coins. Slow-moving, snail-like, they searched the room as he said, 'Balesar, take a loan you're actually able to repay. If you take a farming loan, will you be able to pay it off?' He almost laughed, but then, thinking about what he'd said, he asked softly, 'How much do you need?'

'Twenty thousand.'

'But before taking such a sum, you'll need to show me four or five thousand and put it on this table. Can you?'

'Babu, we are poor labourers. How can we spend so much money?'

'Then how have you come here for a loan? Loans are not as easy as sowing seeds.'

'But, sir, many people in our village have received loans. Poor just like us.'

Sumer Singh didn't want to argue; a crowd of people was gathering. He decided to evade Balesar by asking him to come later. 'Okay, you come in five or six days. I will talk to the BDO.'

And Balesar left, swinging between hope and despair. Outside, the heat was still scorching. It was 4 p.m. In the heat, he felt as if he couldn't even look up in god's direction. He covered his face with his gamcha and set off towards home.

The journey home ground him to dust. Every bone chirped and popped as if it would break out of his body. He reached for his back and stroked his spine. Thinking about how nice it would be if someone could take his broken body and put the pieces back together, he remembered Gulabo. If Gulabiya had been close, the pain wouldn't have bothered him as much. She would slowly stroke away the ache from every knot in his body with her soft hands. But she wasn't with him today. Then, Balesar thought that if she wasn't with him today, she would be tomorrow. Not for an hour or two, or a day or two, but for the rest of their lives. His mind wandered down this path, and soon the pain subsided. In its place, he felt the touch of a soft, tender hand.

4

One day passed after another, and the whole week went by. Today was the day Sumer Singh would meet him. How Balesar had survived these days, only he knew. He'd counted the days on his fingers, twenty-five times a day. Today, his face glowed with happiness and hope. He woke up at dawn, finished his chores, and then tied up some sattu in his gamcha before setting off for the block. He knew that as the sun rose higher, the heat would become sharp and unbearable; it was better to wait outside the block for three hours than burn in the fire.

Bada Babu appeared as soon as the block opened, but Balesar remained outside. He didn't know if it was right for him to be the first to enter the office. While he waited, Bada Babu's office filled up with people. Only after he was done talking to them did he call Balesar in. Balesar entered the office with hope and expectation, hands folded.

'So, Balesar, you work at Patel Singh's farm, right?'

'Yes, hujoor, I was a worker there.'

'And you're a manager now?'

'Yes, I was, but I don't work there anymore.'

'From what I know, Patel didn't just make you the manager; he also gave you a lot of amenities and perks, didn't he? So why do you need a loan?'

'Hujoor, I want to buy an acre or two of land now and farm there.'

'Well. It's true what they say. No matter what one does for a worker, it's never enough. Loosen your grip just a bit, and he'll try to sit on top of your head. Well, nothing is lost yet. Don't leave the job. Go back and work on the farms. I'm saying this for your own good. You'll find deliverance where your ancestors' navels are buried.* Don't get sucked into the whirlpool of these loans. You won't make it out.'

'No, hujoor. I'm not going to work for him anymore. If the loan goes through, I can be the owner of my own farm.' Balesar said, his face shining with faith.

Despite Sumer Singh's attempts to make him understand, Balesar remained determined. Finally, the

---

* Refers to a cultural practice in Bihar, where the umbilical cord of a newborn is buried in a place considered sacred or significant for the family.

enraged Bada Babu said, 'Fine then. I told you. Put five thousand rupees on this table, and then we can talk about a loan.'

Balesar was scared, but he folded his hands once again and said, 'Hujoor, I've said before, we're poor people. Where do we get all this money? If people like you become incensed by us, we'll die in poverty. You know my owner, Patel Singh. I've done backbreaking work for him for years, hujoor. If you try, I can get this loan for sure, sir. Please.'

But all this begging fell on deaf ears.

5

Dutta Babu saw Balesar's determined face and asked, 'But where are you off to now?'

'I'm going to meet this village's mukhiya, Patel Singh, who owns the farm I work on. I'm going to ask him for a loan. I'll talk to you after that,' Balesar said, rolling his eyes.

Dutta Babu was surprised to hear this. He immediately began to prepare a monologue. A serious one. Balesar could tell because Dutta Babu was fussing with his sleeves. He rolled them up and then down and then up and down and up and down and up and down. After ten repetitions, he was satisfied with his sleeves; he then fixed his glasses five times. Then he took a pause and began. 'Are you mad? Why are you going to talk to Patel Singh? Think about it for a minute. If Sumer Singh didn't give you a loan, why on earth would Patel Singh? You know better than I do the state of caste and class discrimination in this country. It's futile for you to try. In my opinion, you only have one way left to obtain a loan.' Saying all of this in a single breath was too taxing for Dutta Babu, who was now hyperventilating. He'd developed breathing problems in the last year. The interval in which he stopped to catch his breath was unbearable for Balesar, who grew more impatient by the minute to know how and when he could get his loan.

A ray of hope on Balesar's face, he asked anxiously, 'Where? Where is that, Dutta Babu?'

Dutta Babu finally caught his breath and put his arm on Balesar's shoulder to steady himself. 'Balesar, I knew your father and his father, too. Their lives were spent on Bhumi Babu's doorstep, working, taking loans, and paying them back. Why don't you go and ask him for a loan? I know that he'll definitely give you one, he's in the business of mahajani. You don't have to pay him a bribe to take a loan either. He knows your family. Forget the villagers, people from the entire district come to borrow money from him. Thanks to his usury, he has a palace for a home. When I need a lakh or two, Bhumi Babu is the only one who can get it done.'

This got through to Balesar. Maybe Dutta Babu was right. *My father married off my aunt using a loan from Bhumi Babu*. He had overheard his parents discussing this as a very young boy. He decided that he'd go to Bhumi Babu. Whatever money he needed, he'd borrow from him.

The very next day, he was at Bhumi Chacha's house – well, it was more of a palace than a house. Even Patel Singh didn't have a house as big as Bhumi's. *Dutta Babu is right; he's made a lot of money in this trade.* He seemed to own a bigha of land at the very least. He thought to himself that if he succeeded in banana farming, he too could have a house like this one day. A palace surrounded by sheesham trees on all sides. *The rangoli-covered walls are so lovely. Dada said that artisans were probably brought in specially for this.* There was a huge staircase in front of the house; up those stairs was a grand verandah. Here, in the verandah, was a seating area where Bhumi Babu and his munshi ji sat. Balesar had been here several times as a child with his grandfather and father. Bhumi Babu was well known in the village. All this came rushing back to him.

Bhumi Babu was a tall, muscular, light-skinned man. *He's so white, it's as if he bathes in milk daily.* God didn't just give him colour, his features were striking, too. Big round eyes to go with a large prominent nose and a regal moustache. You couldn't tell he was a loan shark by looking at him.

When Balesar crossed the stairs and reached Bhumi

Babu, the aggressive out-thrust of his hand startled the moneylender, who was shocked to see him so close. But within the next moment, his expression changed to one of dispassionate neutrality. It didn't take long for Bhumi Babu to understand that this man was here to ask him for something. Bhumi Babu tried to appear preoccupied, as if he didn't have the time to speak just then. But Balesar had made his mind up before setting out that day: he wouldn't leave before securing a loan. If he had to keep sitting there, he would sit there. For this, he was willing to fall at Bhumi Babu's feet. What would happen if he did? Generations have spent their lives beneath the feet of such people. *If I touch his feet, so what?* Without thinking anything more, Balesar flung himself before Bhumi Baba. Bhumi Babu jerked his feet from Balesar's grip. Then, tenderly, he asked, 'Balesar? What's the matter?'

With some hesitation, Balesar responded, 'Yes, maalik. I want to farm my own land.'

'But you work on Patel Singh's land, right? Then what is all this farming business you're talking about?'

'I want to do my own farming now,' said Balesar with building conviction.

'Do you realize how much money you need for a farm? Moreover, farming isn't a one- or two-month seasonal affair. You have to work year-round. You won't be able to farm like that for long. From the outside, having your own farm may look great, Balesar, but when you're actually in it, you'll begin to understand the turmoil at its core. All this farming business is for big people. Only people to whom money means nothing can do it. They put all their savings into it, and only then do they manage to earn something in a year. Seed prices are touching the skies, Balesar!'

Catching on to Balesar's state of mind, Bhumi Babu went in for a last-ditch effort. 'I'm telling you, you must forget this and stay on at Patel Singh's farm. Work hard managing it and earn your bread.'

Balesar, who was listening to Bhumi Babu's words intently, didn't let them bury his hope. Deepening his resolve, he said, 'Whatever happens, maalik, now I want to do my own farming. You lent money to my father and grandfather; they paid off the loan. I will get your money back to you too.'

Bhumi Babu could see that Balesar wouldn't leave him alone, so he made a final attempt to put an end to Balesar's pleas. 'Oh, Balesar. It was a different matter with them. They spent their lives working off the loan at my doorstep. They were people of solid constitutions, able to work both on the farm and in my home. Even in your youth, your body is already that of an ailing old man.

Even if I wanted to give you a loan, I couldn't extract my money by putting you to work. What can you do for me here? And I can't give you any other work either, Balesar. So you tell me, why should I give you a loan?'

'But I give you my word that whatever money I make from farming, it'll go towards paying off the loan,' Balesar repeated himself.

'Listen, Balesar, you can't put your faith in farming. You never know what will and won't happen in a year. At least don't try to get me to put my faith in things from the uncertain future. What will happen in Kosi Ma's flood, who knows? Some people's homes, farms, everything will sink into the water, but even the gods don't have that written anywhere. Don't you know that in your village, Semapur, Nityanand's banana farms were washed away in the storm and flood? What could Nityanand do? You aren't borrowing money in the future; you're borrowing it now. What assurances can you give me?' Bhumi Babu finished talking in circles and placed this plainly before him.

After much deliberation, Balesar stayed firm. Whatever happened, he'd find a way to get the money. He thought for a while about possible solutions and then, with resolve, said, 'Mortgage my land and home. When my money's made, release me.'

Bhumi Babu couldn't believe that Balesar was ready to mortgage his land and home. But hearing the idea of taking on the land as collateral, rice began to puff and pop in his mind. To hide the thoughts crackling about in his brain and to make sure, he asked, 'Are you just saying this to win my trust? Don't go back on your word tomorrow.'

'Okay, maalik. If you can't believe my words, then put it in writing and take your assurance.'

On Bhumi Babu's indication, Munshi ji took an ink pad and a blank sheet of paper from the drawer and extended them towards Balesar. He reached out towards the page with an inked thumb, but as he approached the paper, his thumb froze.

Bhumi Babu immediately understood what was on Balesar's mind. He said, 'Listen, Balesar, think about it once again. I'd never involve my ancestral home and land in a loan scheme. People would rather die than sell or mortgage their home.'

Balesar heard what Bhumi Babu had to say, concealing his inner doubts, and quickly replied, 'No, maalik, no. I was just thinking about where I should make my thumb impression on this blank page.' Balesar followed Munshi ji's directions and placed his kohl print on the page. When he was finally satisfied, Bhumi Babu opened his cash box, counted out 20,000 five times by hand, and then handed it to Munshi ji to recount. Munshi ji counted the money thrice, wetting his fingers with his tongue. After this, Bhumi Babu handed the money over to Balesar, saying, 'So, Balesar, count it thoroughly.' As Balesar counted the notes, Bhumi Babu kept his piercing gaze fixed on the cash.

Finally, after so many days, Balesar's desire had been fulfilled. Getting the money, a look of relief washed over his face. Thoughts racing, he stowed the cash securely in his waistband and set off towards home. After many days, his bed, which had felt like a bed of thorns, seemed as soft as cotton.

Balesar kept touching the money around his waist and thought, *I must keep this money carefully. If Gulabiya had been there today, she would have kept it safe.* Every time, Gulabiya's absence pierced Balesar's heart. *But, if not today, then tomorrow, Gulabiya will be the queen of my life.* In his mind's eye, he envisioned Gulabiya, adorned with flowers, descending queen-like from on high. He would earn his fortune banana farming. Balesar would be a powerful seth and Gulabiya his sethani. Lost in this colourful dream, Balesar didn't know when sleep took him.

—

Since the day Balesar took on the loan and got the money, the worries on his mind had increased. At thirty, Balesar's eyes shimmered with dreams that a fifty-year-old would usually nurture. Every day, he dreamt of banana farming. Not an ordinary harvest, but an excellent one. Thinking of a successful harvest gave him happiness. He thought of Deepak Ghosh and Harik Sanyal. They rented out fertile land. Deepak Ghosh's land was excellent and alluvial. He had thirty bighas of land in Semapur. There were two–three places where he had land. Some in Bavangunj and some in Sakreli. *I think I will rent land in Bavangunj. The land in Bavangunj is excellent. After farming all these years, I know that you need alluvial soil for banana farming. I have gone to Bavangunj to work the fields several times for Patel Singh. I'm familiar with the fields there. So let me take one or two bighas of land from Deepak Ghosh. I'll give half the money now and the other half later, after the harvest. And as for equipment, tractors are easy to find nearby, from Muddar saav or Tanti Ram.* In this manner, Balesar began keeping a ledger of accounts in his head. Tractors were expensive. He'd get a mechanical–manual machine from Muthri or Sitaram instead. He could speak to Mangru, who knew them. Saplings he'd get from Motilal Babu. He'd find the ones that were flexible in the middle but had solid, strong roots. The leaves would be sword-like and sharp. Motilal Babu sold that kind of plant. Deep in thought now, Balesar enumerated all the farmers' banana varietals. Malbhog, Amritsagar, Champa, Chinese Champa, Alpana, Bheemkela, Nendran. *But, I think, for me, just Alpana and Malbhog.*

When it came to nitrogen, potash, and phosphorus for the fields, and which would be best for profits, he would have to ask Motilal Babu, who was a very experienced farmer. After asking Motilal Babu what ratio to look for, he'd go and get the nitrogen and potash. He might end up needing phosphorus too, but he'd need nitrogen and potash for sure. *Anyway, it's my first year of farming, so I'll adjust water and fertilizer according to the plant. I know I have to leave about one-and-a-half bitta of space around each banana tree's trunk, and make strips between the rows of half bitta. I can do all this work on my own.* For irrigation, he could borrow Dayanand Babu's pumping set-up. He could use Gulabiya's help, but Gulabiya worked at Nityanand Babu's farm… Balesar began thinking ahead.

As time goes on, the plants will grow beyond just needing fertilizer, which is all I know about. Gulabiya and I could farm together, be caretakers of our land together. All I know about taking care of banana saplings is that as they grow, one must cut leaves from the middle. Gulabiya has a brilliant understanding of all this. Balesar knew that the utmost care was needed in banana farming. No sooner had one planted saplings than children would begin to spring up. These children would divide the soil's nutrients. But no matter. *Whenever that happens, my Gulabo and I can do the cutting together.*

Much better than my farming knowledge is Gulabiya's. I mostly get fertilizer and seeds. I don't work much on the farm, but Gulabiya could handle this well. We'll work really hard, Gulabo and I, and according to our own taste, we'll plant grasses as far as we can see, waving and shifting in the wind.

Thinking of green leaves, Balesar's heart was more verdant and lush than is possible to say. All around, thriving crops.

And on the field he had rented, stalks began shooting up. Gulabo, seeing this, asked, 'Are you just going to stand and stare and admire your banana stalks? Have you arranged tractors to sell all these? The stems have burst through the soil like your youth.' Balesar ignored this playful jibe, so she changed tack. 'Well, it's the first time you've farmed your own crop. Now buy bamboo from Urma's father to support the stalks. He will give you good bamboo, and at a cheap rate,' explained Gulabo.

And, in the blink of an eye, five months passed. The bananas were doing very well. Balesar was astonished. He was lost in this feeling one day when Gulabo, lightly running a finger across his cheek, said, 'Don't be so astounded. After all, it's our hard work that's bearing fruit. It's on everybody's lips: the amazing farming Gulabo and Balesar are doing together. Wah, Balesar, wah.'

Balesar thought Gulabo would go on in this manner, so he answered, 'No, Gulabo, no. This flourishing, all this cheer, it's the result of your blood and sweat. The cheer of your spirit gave us plants and fruit.'

Balesar began to dream of a truck parked near the field. They wouldn't even negotiate under hundred rupees per bundle. Not only that, the trucker would also be willing to agree at a fantastically high price. They'd have their crops in trucks everywhere. *Kolkata, Benares, Uttar Pradesh, Patna, and Azamgarh's businesspeople will buy our crops.* Emotions overcame Balesar. He began to imagine that whatever price he set today, businesspeople would pay. But he wouldn't do anything without asking Gulabo.

He went over to be close to Gulabo, standing in a corner of the field.

She was looking at the saplings and bushes she'd planted very carefully. Balesar interrupted her, touching the sword-like leaves, and asked, 'You have planted this vegetable leaf tree. Would a fruit trader take this?'

Gulabo's reply came immediately. 'What do I have to do with a trader? This plant of mine can only be taken by a trader who is mine. The one who is the trader of my body and soul.'

Hearing Gulabo's words, Balesar thought he would burst into laughter from joy. Later, when his dreams were shattered, he would look back on this moment and really laugh. A deep, loud laugh at this memory would echo everywhere.

6

Everyone saw, everyone watched Gulabiya and Balesar's hard work. Just as in Balesar's dreams, his farming dazzled every farmer in Semapur. After taking two bighas of land from Deepak Ghosh, he and Gulabiya had begun planting in the fields. Since that day, Gulabiya had tilled this soil, soaking it in her blood and sweat. Before the sowing, Balesar went with Gulabiya to the Shiv Mandir, the one Satyanarayan Jaiswal had made in the memory of his parents.

It was there that, as instructed by Gulabiya, Balesar conducted a puja that even some of the most prominent men of the village might not have managed. Incense, frankincense, sandalwood – Gulabiya ordered all this. Having ordered everything, however, in the end she went to the market herself and picked out each item. After all, it was her own home's puja. They engaged a priest who would recite the Sanskrit verses perfectly. That would please the gods. If the mantra was wrong, would the gods bless them with wealth and success?

On that same day, Gulabo stopped working for Nityanand Babu. After the puja at the temple, Balesar sprinkled the blessed soil in every field. Gulabiya prayed with sincerity over every field. After they'd completed their puja, the two ploughed the farm together. From that day on, the two of them completely committed themselves as a unit to farming, the way one tends to and nurtures their own children.

A month or two passed. The field was ready for cultivation. Monsoon was about to begin. Balesar had already brought seedlings from Motilal Babu and planted them. Gulabo knew that Balesar only planted saplings of his own choosing, so she stuck to planting her vegetable cultivar saplings at the corners of each field.

Time passed swiftly before their eyes. Green leaves had already sprouted from the seedlings. Gulabiya put all her experience to good use in this field. As soon as a few leaves came out, she'd run about, spraying them with nitrogen and phosphorus. Gulabiya did not need to go to a tree doctor or specialist to do all this. She'd been working in the fields since she was a child, twenty years of her life. Balesar would sit in his field and watch Gulabiya. And Gulabiya, she spent her whole day absorbed in her work. She had no time to do anything but work. What to do with each plant, when to give it medicine, when to cut its leaves, when to give it a drink of water, when to prune the seedlings, Gulabiya alone took care of all this.

Balesar looked at his billowing green fields with wonderment. He was amazed at the way Gulabo had managed all this work single-handedly. He thought to himself, in amazement, *Gulabo doesn't let the burden of the work fall on me, not even the slightest bit. There's no work Gulabo hasn't done. Look at the field, the way it looks. If I had done it myself, it wouldn't have flourished the way it has under her hands. It's Gulabo who gives this field more love, more than if it were her own child. She doesn't think about her body or her comfort. It's as if she dissolves into the work, totally without consciousness of anything but the field. If I try to lend a hand, she holds my hand and moves it aside. She always says the same thing: 'Don't touch my little children. I'm raising them with such care. When they grow up, you can play with them.'*

Balesar considered this with deep seriousness. He tried to understand what she meant. He grasped a little of the meaning, but as soon as he tried to capture it in his mind, a tickling sensation would arise in his chest. His mind would wander about endlessly, and take him to the fields and meadows of their childhood, where they would go out to graze goats.

Gulabiya would take out everything she'd brought from home and place it in front of me. She would keep saying that we will eat together. Whatever we've brought, let's combine everything. But she'd barely eat anything; in the course of conversation, she'd end up making me eat, saying that she'd heard that boys always felt very hungry. Since then, I've never been able to hide anything from her.

With my mother working house to house as a maid, it was very difficult to keep our stomachs full. We were fortunate that my father left home to work in Punjab and returned with enough money to build us a house. Since then, Gulabo was a regular visitor to our house.

Then, Balesar's mother passed away, and Gulabo was flowering into a young woman on the brink of puberty. Her daily visits had come to an end. Today, he watched that same Gulabo, completely devoted to farming. *As if the fields belong to her, and so do I.* Balesar shivered with anticipation at this thought. Soon, it would all be true. With shining eyes, he admired Gulabiya as she swayed like a tender banana leaf in his fields.

7

And so every day, Gulabo, after working in her fields, would be separated from Balesar, the way a chakwa separates from a chakai. All night, they would yearn for each other, with a kind of pain neither had ever experienced before.

So Gulabo came to the field every day with double the enthusiasm. Her arrival as inevitable as the earth meeting the sky. Just as Kosi Ma leaves the Himalayas and runs in the direction of the Ganges, so would Gulabiya run towards Balesar's fields. And then once they met, they'd be together the whole day. Time kept passing at a fast pace. As they watched, the trees burst into bloom. Gulabo was very happy to see this, because the yield in the first year was rarely as robust as this. Balesar said to Gulabo, 'All of this, this wonderful result, is because of your hard work and insight, Gulabo.' Taking Gulabo's hand in his, he lovingly touched a finger to her cheek, tracing words on it, and continued, 'Gulabo, all that we've accomplished in farming is because of your love. Look how beautifully this love has blossomed. To tell you the truth, Gulabo, if we cultivate this successfully for four or five years, we'll be lakhpatis. No one else in the village has such flourishing crops. Once these flowers fatten up, we'll be able to auction our crop, just you watch.'

Gulabo and Balesar talk about things like this all day, and wild dreams bloom in Gulabo's head. Wild, syrupy. Full of the maddeningly intoxicating scent and syrup of mahua.

And soon, four months pass. Ten more days before the month of Sawan arrives. Gulabiya and Balesar have been anxiously staring down the long tunnel of summer, waiting for the rains at the other end. Several times, clouds have descended with crisp rain, but the real rain comes with Sawan. When Sawan descends, the fields and farms will become fragrant with the perfume of blooming banana flowers. And indeed, as Sawan descended, Balesar's fields were filled with scent. Ready for sale. Everyone had their eyes on his fields. And every farmer, from small plot-owners to large landholders, repeated the same thing: 'Whatever happens, you'll make a lot of profit, Balesar.'

And all this, travelling from ear to ear, reached Patel Singh's – Balesar's farming had turned out really well. Patel Singh was the mukhiya of the village, and he would not tolerate anyone praising one of *his* labourers in front of him. *I mean, do these people have any respect or not? It's as if Balesar is making faces at me, humiliating me.* His brain was racing, thinking of what he should do next. First of all, he had to find out how Balesar had managed this miracle. Once he did, he realized who all had helped Balesar on his way.

Patel Babu, the mukhiya. He never crosses the line, but today he has to. It wasn't just about him; it was for Bhumi Babu's benefit too. It was useless to allow these small people to sit on your head. The sheikh of Pachhiari Tola had kept Birna of Chamartoli on his head for many years, and in the end, the same Birna formed a union and destroyed all of Sheikh Babu's land. Overnight, they cut down all the crops. They didn't think for a moment about the fact that Sheikh Babu had taken care of their households, not for months but for years. If the others looted, let them loot, but at least Birna shouldn't have done that. Who knows what else Patel Babu was thinking. *If this Balesar is not stopped, he will sit on our heads.* Today, Patel Singh had sprained his leg. He was thinking about all this while strolling on his porch. If he sent the news to

Bhumi Babu's house, Bhumi Babu may dismiss it. After all, he was a moneylender. *He may earn a lot of money, but I am the village's mukhiya. Everyone has their time. I accept that I'm the landlord and the mukhiya, and he the mahajan. But the scriptures tell us that when the time comes, one must act and speak up. He who does this is the clever pundit.* He must go to Bhumi Babu immediately. He wouldn't delay a moment longer. Almost unconsciously, his feet began taking him towards Bhumi Babu's house. Many people were surprised to see him walking about. Patel Singh, who has never moved a step without a horse and carriage cavalcade, is walking around on foot! No one could understand what was going on. The more people who saw, the more the confusion grew.

Steadily walking, Patel Singh arrived at Bhumi Babu's door. Holding his dhoti, he shouted out, 'Hey, Bhumi Babu, where are you? Are you there or not?' Bhumi Babu, who had been sitting in his office busy with his ledgers, sprang up on hearing Patel Singh's voice. He got off his cushion and rushed outside. He stared at Patel Singh, standing at his threshold. Fixing the folds of his dhoti, he clambered down and bowed to Patel Singh with folded hands. A tangled heap of questions in his mind, he managed to blurt out, 'Today you came to my house? If you had sent word, I would have come to you. It is my great fortune that your footsteps have fallen in this house. My house has become holy today.' Perhaps Patel Singh had no interest in all this, because he just walked towards the door. Stopping just short, he asked if Bhumi Babu was only going to thank him at the threshold or ask him to come inside.

Once inside, Bhumi Babu gave a loud yell and screamed at his servant, Sugna, to tidy everything up. Sugna, who had come to the door with Bhumi Babu, hurried upstairs, followed at a relaxed pace by Bhumi Babu and Patel Singh.

At Bhumi Babu's insistence, Patel Singh sat down on a cushion, crossing his legs and making himself comfortable. Without beating around the bush, gritting his teeth, he began, 'Bhumi Babu, you already know what Balesar is – he is a regular labourer on my farm. I had made him the manager of the farm because of his hard work and honesty. What comforts did we not give him? But what can I tell you, if you give these little people something, they will sit on your head. He was such a good manager, and he gave it up. Something possessed him to think that if he wanted to, he could farm on his own. I mean, he ran around looking for a loan from the block and even came to me. When nothing worked out, he approached you, and you gave him a loan without a thought. Now you think for yourself, Bhumi Babu, if a worker can defy me, why wouldn't he do the same to you tomorrow?'

Bhumi Babu's head pounded on hearing these words. 'Yes, I have made a big mistake, but what can be done now?'

Seeing that his throw had hit the mark, Patel Singh kept going, 'Think about it, the land you've based the loan on, what will you do if it slips out of your hands? You don't want to let go of that land. Today, he has cultivated two bighas, tomorrow if he capitalizes on this and cultivates ten, the next day he could become a moneylender. Think about yourself; if he starts doing mahajani, he'll be your competitor. Then the business will be divided between the two of you. I wouldn't want my business to be divided.'

Bhumi Babu began to feel that he really had made a big mistake, and no one but Patel Babu could correct it. In a sad tone, he asked, 'Can this mistake be fixed? If there is something that can be done, if there is a way, please tell me, I'll do whatever you say.'

Patel Babu seemed to have already made up his mind on what had to happen, so he brought his mouth to Bhumi Babu's ear and spoke in a low tone. 'You know that the harvest time is very near. This is the time when

Balesar can be defeated.' Hearing this, Bhumi Babu's wilted expression was wiped off his face. A brightness bloomed on it again, as if a lost bet had been won once more. A glint appeared in his eyes, and he, who had been listening at an arm's length, now drew close to Patel Singh and said, 'Speak, Patel Babu, speak. What should I do to wound him?' Patel Babu was right, thought Bhumi; he should start doing something for himself. No matter what happened now, he would not let Balesar move forward.

Patel Babu told him the method to beat Balesar. 'Balesar's crops are now completely ready for harvest. There are four days to Sawan. Traders are touring everyone's fields. They are looking at all the fields and listening for any information. Everyone's crop, good or bad, is ready. But when the traders see Balesar's field, they turn away from all the others. Every once in a while, amongst the poor, a beautiful woman comes along, and all the men's eyes are drawn to her. That's what is happening with Balesar's banana field. And, you know, don't you, that the secret behind his flourishing farm is Jogbaniya's sister, Gulabiya? It's thanks to that girl's hands and head that things are bursting forth with youthful vigour in Balesar's field. So, if you defeat Balesar at one place, at another place she'll defeat you.'

Bhumi Babu was staring at Patel Babu with big-big eyes that repeated one question. 'Tell me, what should be done?'

Patel Babu squeezed his hands together five times before replying. 'What you have to do is provoke all the traders against him with the force of money, such that no one buys bananas from him. Set the price at half the market rate. Make it so that, forget the price for his crop, he won't even get a decent price for the field.'

'I understand. I understand everything,' said Bhumi Babu. 'And as far as Gulabiya is concerned, we'll make some other arrangements. As long as this midget follows Balesar, luck remains with him. Now, Balesar's farm will go to ruin, and Gulabiya will go to her husband's house. I will call Jogbaniya tomorrow and tell him to tie his sister to the feet of a man, or I will tie up that Jogbaniya and beat him. Bhumi Babu, when Gulabiya goes to her sasural, Balesar's luck goes to hell. As soon as Gulabiya is married, he will go mad and die.'

With that, Patel Babu started guffawing. And seeing his honour and reputation safe, Bhumi Babu joined in.

8

And so, Balesar's farm was finished. From the day Gulabiya stopped coming to Balesar's fields, they were destroyed. Gulabiya was that farm's Goddess Laxmi, a true Laxmi; if there was no Gulabiya, there would be no prosperity, because Laxmi resided in Gulabiya's feet. From the day Gulabiya had devoted her life and energy to the farm, it was as if Laxmi was walking across the fields, leaving her auspicious footsteps behind.

Gulabiya had not been to the field for days. What could have happened? Balesar sat in thought, but it was as though his brain had stopped working. He would look here, he would look there. It was eerie, ghostly, in the empty fields. No one to look at him, no voice to call for him. Just him, walking his fields. He wandered aimlessly, looking for someone to ask about Gulabo. All alone, he could only ask himself questions. What on earth could have happened to her? Could her body and soul not be in it anymore? She had worked these fields like no one else ever would or could. If she was unwell, she would definitely have sent word. *No, no, Gulabo hasn't given up on this*, Balesar prayed silently.

But then, what had happened? In the past, not only birds but people, too, had chirped on these fields. Now, each day it felt more and more as if these fields were not fields at all – they had become a barren, desolate wasteland. And in this valley of death, bodies burnt – slowly, softly smouldering. Balesar could not escape the enveloping fire. As a flame rises from a burning corpse, a flame licked at Balesar's heart. Why did he not get up? *It's not just about Gulabiya; it's a question of these fields as well.* Balesar knew whose hand was behind the devaluation of his crop, but no one in the village would speak up. He was afraid to speak up if his was the lone voice. What if his suspicions were false? But Balesar believed in his heart that it was not a lie. Bhumi Babu was no less guilty of destroying his farm than Patel Babu.

It felt as if the banana trees were not bearing fruit anymore, corpses standing upright at a cremation ground. Each tree was like a man crying over his fate. Balesar's heart cried out in pain with them. What had happened to his fields? A short while ago, everyone had seen this as Laxmi's abode. And now, it was a cremation ground. Thinking about this was tiring to Balesar, more and more tiring. A scene from four days ago came to him, as if it were happening again at that very moment.

Bhumi Babu had come to the fields with ten lathi-wielding enforcers and said, 'What, Balesar, it's been over a year since you took the money from me. In the agreement, you had written that you'd return everything, interest included, within the year. I've been expecting you to come to me for a long time. I thought that once your banana crop was sold, I'd see some return. But even after you've sold your crop, I haven't gotten the scent of a penny. And now I can't wait any longer.' Bhumi Babu had gone on, but Balesar's ears could not hear a thing. His body had turned to stone. Like a stone idol – still, motionless. Finally, with much exertion, he managed to speak.

Embarrassed and hesitant, he had said to Bhumi Babu, 'Maalik, the crop that was supposed to make a forty- or fifty-thousand-rupee profit, the traders priced it at twenty thousand. And not just one trader, all the traders. I'd barely managed to hold the cash in my hands for a moment before the landowner and the fertilizer supplier came and took their dues. You were thinking about getting your money; now all I can say is that I've lost my house.'

In response, Bhumi Babu put on an expression of anger and said, 'Oh, Balesar, what shall I do with that graveyard of yours? Bury my dead? And now I can't even recover my money by selling it. I'll have to satisfy myself with this death valley.' And so, Bhumi Babu had left the field, red with rage.

Each of these little scenes played before Balesar's eyes, one by one.

As if worrying and wondering about Gulabo wasn't bad enough, on top of that, he now had to worry about the debt as well. All these blows had fallen on him at once. How could he bear it? He was broken, from top to bottom. According to the words on Bhumi Babu's loan agreement, Balesar's house and home were finished.

It wasn't right to leave the raw crop in the field for long; the bananas would ripen right there on the stalk, so Balesar had to sell off his crop in desperation. The harvest from which he would have made a profit of fifty thousand rupees had been sold for eighteen or twenty thousand.

And from that day on, Balesar had become unaware of everyone. He was no longer conscious of his body or his life. He let his clothes become filthy. The very same Balesar Babu, who yesterday had taken great care of his appearance, today looked like a poor ascetic. Now he didn't know where he would bathe, where he would live. He had no home to live in and no money for food or drink.

Wealth was leaving him as it does when Laxmi leaves a house. It is said that just as Laxmi arrives slowly, she also leaves the home slowly. But he did not know by which door his Laxmi had come and by which door she had left. From the day Gulabo came to his house, all the happiness came along with her. And the day Gulabo disappeared, all the joy seemed to have vanished. Balesar remembered that Gulabo had stopped coming to the field eight days before the crop was to be sold. When Laxmi had stopped coming, how could her blessings come from the crop?

In the end, Gulabiya didn't come. Balesar lived a strange, troubled life. He would go to the field for a while, and stare at his barren banana trees, then descend, like a dark storm cloud, on the Thakurwari.

Now Balesar just sits at the Thakurwari. He sits at the door of the mandir. Again and again, he stares at the Thakurwari with empty eyes. He mutters something to himself. No one can understand.

If Balesar knew what he was muttering, he would have tried to explain himself. Looking at him, it wasn't clear if he himself understood what he was babbling.

Balesar longed to go inside and hug god and wail. But his legs didn't move. He remembered the day Gulabiya had put her head on his chest and said, 'May this shadow of mine never leave my life.' Balesar had replied that all that was left to be done was the harvesting. After that, in this very Thakurwari, he would apply sindoor to the parting of her hair. But none of this happened.

When he sold the crop at a loss, he was going to Gulabiya's house, burdened with sorrow. Maybe he would find some peace and relief there. But this could not happen. On his way there, he met his older bhouji, who asked him, 'Where are you going, Deor?' though she knew where he would be going alone at that hour. That day, Balesar decided not to hide anything. He said, with a clear mind, 'I am going to see Gulabo.' His sister-in-law told him that Gulabo had left their village as a married woman. Balesar was struck senseless.

Bhouji then told him the entire story. 'I don't know what spirit possessed Jogbaniya. One day, he started beating poor Gulabiya, and kept at it for two whole hours. He kept her at home by force, but Gulabiya remained stubborn, insisting she would go to meet you. Her insistence was in vain. One day, Gulabo tried to break the door latch and escape, but was caught. After that, Bhoujayi Bimli pushed her back into the house and tied her hands and feet. Jogbaniya was under strict orders not to let her go anywhere.

'People were saying a lot of things. Pudniya's mother whispered in my ear that Jogbaniya had been paid to have his sister's hands stained yellow in bridal turmeric and send her out of the village as soon as possible, and to do this so quickly that the news wouldn't spread from ear to ear, otherwise the whole village would shun Jogbaniya. This was the rumour in the air.

'Gulabiya was tied up for four or five days. She gave up food and water. If Bhoujayi tried to feed her, she'd spit everything out and then spit at her. For a day or two, she cursed and cursed Bhoujayi. Gulabo understood everything. She knew her family was doing all this on someone else's orders. Bhoujayi Bimli ignored her. She knew Gulabo's words carried no weight. All this was a temporary fever, not a seasonal one that would keep returning. This was the fever people called influenza, which would come over someone for a day or two. Once the fever subsided, one would slowly recover. After all, how long could she go on cursing her? She had given up food. How many will have the energy to keep screaming and shouting when they are hungry and thirsty? And Bhoujayi was right. After a day or two, Gulabo stopped talking and cursing. With time, the strength left her body. Once or twice, she even fainted.

'If she fainted while tied up, Bhoujayi released her from her restraints and laid her on the khatiya. Gulabo said nothing. What could she have said? Her body was broken and shattered. She just opened her numb, unseeing eyes sometimes and stared. When people saw her, they said she was holding on to life in the hope that someone would come for her.

'It must have been three or four days later that she was married off to her cousin, Basant. Really, it was hardly a wedding; Basant just came and marked her with sindoor. By that time, Gulabiya's body and mind had become useless. She had no awareness of what was happening. Well, everything that was happening in the house was just a play, planned and organized. And the main actors in this play were Jogbaniya and Bimli.

'All of Gulabo's hopes and dreams were washed away in a stream of blood. She was entirely unconscious. Basant had become the master of her life without her even realizing it. Had she had any consciousness, she wouldn't have let all this happen. But it did, everything Gulabo could never have imagined happened. Some distant relatives who lived in the neighbourhood must have come to sing for the wedding, but inwardly, everyone must have been afraid and unsettled.'

Bhouji paused a little, then said, 'Is a wedding like this really even a wedding? How good it would have been if Gulabo's baraat came dressed up, singing and dancing. Gulabo was the only girl in the village who was both beautiful and intelligent and good at everything she did. How wonderful it would have been if this girl's in-laws were from this village. What can I say, Deor, Dukhni Nani said that Gulabo was not a bride leaving on her doli, but a corpse being carried away. They took her away at night, in the silent darkness. There was not a chirp from the birds. But yes, many people say that they heard a piercing scream in the middle of the night. That scream was none other than Gulabiya's. She was screaming your name, Deor. Oh, Deor, the one you're going to has already been taken away by someone else.' Bhouji's eyes filled with tears, her voice trembling. In a tearful tone, she added, 'Whatever it may be, the words of important people carry weight. Look at what all these big people can get done just because they have taken a slight hit.

Had she been aware, all this would have made Gulabiya miserable. Now, Bimli Bhouji has dealt with the situation by force, but what she did was not right. We'll spend all our days under the weight of these boys. Think about it, Balesar, today this happened to Gulabo, tomorrow it could happen to anyone else. These big men don't want to see anyone's happiness get in the way of their money. They just want everything for themselves. No one should get ahead of them in money or in prestige. Look what happened to you. You didn't want to equal them, you just wanted to make some money for yourself. And what did you get? Neither money nor love. Both things went away together. We little people should have no minds of our own, no desires, no dreams; we should have no ambitions when it comes to clashing with big people. They are willing to crush us. What these big people wouldn't do for money!'

Balesar remembered everything; one by one, things came to him. For the next ten days, he had stood at Patel Babu and Bhumi Babu's doors. For minutes on end, he would just stand and stare at them with questioning eyes, saying nothing. Some days, he would go to the banana fields and sob, or go to the Thakurwari and bang his head at the threshold. Now, after weeping for so long, the tears in his eyes had dried up. Even after banging his head on the threshold, he no longer felt any pain. Balesar's body and limbs had become entirely numb.

He didn't think about eating, didn't think about drinking. He neither cared about his appearance nor his body. Without Gulabiya, Balesar's place in the world was meaningless. A living corpse standing on the cremation ground.

9

Gulabiya opened her eyes in a house that wasn't hers. It was entirely unfamiliar to her. Opening her eyes wide, she frantically scanned the house, the door – she couldn't recognize a thing. After a few days spent unconscious, her body was worn out, but she gathered all the strength she had and came out to the courtyard. She carefully examined everything. She recognized nothing, nothing here belonged to her. She rubbed her eyes, trying to identify something, anything, but it was hopeless. She looked at the vanity – some of her things had been kept there. Hanging over it was a photo. *But who the hell is that*? She had no idea.

She began screaming loudly, 'Where have you brought me, you burnt-face bastards?' Her screams brought out her groom, Basant.

He grabbed her violently by the wrist, twisting it as he said, 'What are you screaming for, you banshee? This is your groom's house. You are at your in-laws' now. This is not your brother's place, where you can yell and shout. There is no one here to hear your screams. Now shut up and go inside.'

But Gulabiya persisted at the same pitch. 'Neither are you my man, nor am I your woman. Who are you to give me orders? How dare you think you have any power over me? You, who have no business with me, not even half a paisa's worth. Your word isn't binding. I am not your slave. Got it?' She tried to free herself and run away, but her weak body fell to the ground, as if overcome by a dizzy spell.

Basant had been tolerating his wife's screaming for a long time, each word striking him as if he were a bronze vessel, until the reverberations had him tingling with anger. Enraged, he grabbed her by both arms and pulled her up, saying in a raised voice, 'You weren't a slave yet because you hadn't met a real man. But from today, you are my slave. And I will order you around. Now open your ears and listen to this – I am now your man. Man, meaning master. From today, you will obey me as your master.'

Gulabiya raised her bowed head and looked at Basant's face in anger. Who knows where she got the strength from, but she said, nearly screeching, 'What proof do you have that you are my husband, and I your wife?'

Hearing this, Basant violently rubbed his fingers along the parting of her hair and said, 'This… this bright red sindoor in your parting is proof that I'm your husband.'

Gulabiya placed a finger on her maang and saw with her own eyes that it was stained red with senoor. Her eyes dulled for a moment before she began to cast about in desperation. Her gaze fell on an aluminium jug, full of water. Snatching it up, she poured from it, over her lowered head. As soon as the water touched it, the senoor began to run, washing away. She scrubbed at her forehead with one hand as she poured water with the other, trying to remove every trace of the vermilion powder. The more she scrubbed, the more bright red rivulets covered her skin, until her face was entirely red. Now, Gulabiya appeared in the form of a vengeful goddess, full of rage. It was as if the red, vivid hibiscus flowers offered to Bhagwati covered her in their deep hue. It looked like she'd slayed someone with her bare hands and was covered in her victim's blood. For a moment, this image caused a fear to take root in Basant's mind, but he quickly suppressed it. Gulabiya's scalp was now barren. Looking at the flowing stream of senoor beneath her feet, she declared, 'I refuse to consider this marriage a marriage. I have washed it away. Forcefully filling someone's parting with senoor does not make a marriage. I have washed it all away: you, the wedding, the vermilion. Now you aren't my master, and I'm not your servant. What evidence do you have now that you're my man and my master?'

Basant, who had been staring at the form Gulabiya had taken, snatched the jug from her hand and threw it aside. 'So what if you wash it off once? Who cares what you think? I'll simply fill your parting again every time you wash the senoor off. Here, I'll fill it now.' Saying this, Basant gathered up the streams of red running down her cheeks in his right palm and placed the colour back onto her head. He didn't just place it; he pressed it in. He did this again and again and again until her forehead was red like the rising sun.

Still in a fit of rage, he said, 'Everyone knows you're my wife now. Do you understand?'

Gulabiya used all her strength to get up. She pushed her hair back from her forehead and grabbed Basant by the collar. 'I'll wipe it off a thousand times. Every time you do it, I'll wipe it off.' Grinding her teeth, she grabbed and pulled at his shirt. She kept pulling, and at the same time, she was screaming with all the power she could muster. All of this screaming had found its way outside the courtyard, and a crowd had gathered. The people of the village had come in excitement to see the new bride; they hadn't expected this spectacle. The women of the neighbourhood stared from behind their veils, rapt. Children watched in amazement, their jaws open, splitting their faces in two, like the relationship between Basant and Gulabiya, which they were witnessing split apart.

Basant grew angrier when he saw the neighbours gathered. He scanned the crowd as he tried to take Gulabiya away. But Gulabiya screamed and screamed, cursing at Basant. 'This man married me against my will! I wasn't conscious when I was married. His saying so won't make me his wife!' The women's gazes oscillated between Basant and Gulabiya. Before she could say anything more, Basant took Gulabiya inside and pushed her down onto the cot. Then he stormed out and locked the room. Gulabo curled up, her body trembling, and sobbed.

Basant's mother, Janaki, had seen everything. 'Leave her in that room, Basant. Let her die of hunger and thirst for two more days. That'll calm her down. How long will she protest? Stronger people have been broken. She's not some Sati, who'll pray for her lover until the end of time. Even Sati didn't end up with her Shiva after all of that. This whore has been a real pain in the neck since she got here. If I'd known all this before, I never would have married my son into this mess. She should have stayed her brother's problem. Bimli has offloaded her onto my head. I don't even know what she said to summon you there, only to throw this disaster on us. This mad, deranged woman. Had Bimli run out of grooms, that she had to trap my son in this? Bimli found no one else to torment; she's done this to her own brother. This witch hexed her own brother. What is this ghastly match?'

Janaki's pitch was loud enough for Gulabo to hear from inside the room. She stopped sobbing and listened intently. After thundering on for an hour and a half, Basant's mother stopped. The commotion outside had quietened. Silence seeped through the house. Gulabiya closed her eyes and went back to the recent past. It played in front of her like a cinema reel.

10

That day, when I was getting ready to go to the field, my brother forbade me from leaving. I brushed him off and started walking out, and this angered Jogbaniya. He grabbed my arm and slapped me across the cheek. I tried to free myself from his grip and run away. I fell. That's when my sister-in-law, Bimli, arrived. She got her claws into me and started dragging me into the house. Oh, I pounced like a tigress and pushed her onto the floor. If Bhaiya hadn't stopped me, I don't know what I would have done to her that day. Even my brother was scared, seeing this side of me. I had become a tumultuous storm, a gale that would uproot the biggest trees. My brother ground his teeth and said, 'From today, you will not go to the farm.'

Enraged, I asked, 'Why?'

Bhaiya answered that question with one of his own. 'Why? Are those your fields that you have to go there? Who is he to you?'

'Who is he to you?' That question stung her. It felt

as though, at the very last moment of her life, she was being asked a piercing question. And now how could she lie? She plainly said, without shame or hesitation, 'If you want to hear it, then listen carefully. Who is Balesar to me? Balesar is the man who is to be my husband. He is the man I will marry. Now hear this. Yes, those are my fields too. All these days, I've fed not only myself but both of you from my work there. You never stopped me then, why are you stopping me now?

'Tell me, is someone else coming to feed you both now? Or are you going to tie me up here and eat the earnings you make selling my body?'

My words sent Bhaiya into an animalistic rage. He grabbed my throat with his paw, like a tiger suffocating its prey, and growled, 'You bitch, how dare you talk about earning money for a man when you're nothing but a woman? If there were fifty women like you in this house, I could feed them on my own. Why would I eat the earnings from your body?' Who knows what Bhaiya might have done to me in his anger. I was lucky that someone chose that very moment to knock on our door.

The knock was Patel Singh. Bhaiya hurried to the door. I listened closely to their conversation.

'Listen, Jogbaniya, keep your sister tied up, so she doesn't cause a commotion. As soon as possible, get her married and send her away from the village. I said this yesterday as well.'

'But, maalik, how will I get her married off on such short notice?'

Patel Singh sounded irritated and replied tersely, 'I don't care how, just get it done. If you can't find anyone, you marry your sister yourself.'

It seemed like my brother's voice had been snatched from his throat. The same bhaiya who had been boasting of his manhood had shrunk and crumpled like a woman when he came face to face with Patel Singh.

Then, voice wavering, he said, 'What are you saying, maalik? Can any Hindu marry his own sister? Why would you say such a sinful thing?' He fell silent.

I don't know why, but in that moment, instead of at Bhaiya, my fury flared up against Patel Singh. I said, 'This poisonous tree must be uprooted – it is spreading its poison to the whole forest.' Patel Singh must have heard me, but I don't know what he was thinking. He remained silent. When Bhaiya came back in, he was carrying something in his waistband. It must have been a wad of cash. Patel Singh must have given it to my brother to sell me off.

'Arre, you are hardly a man. You're a disgrace to men. For money, you'll sell anything and everything. In front of money, you turn into a dog, licking your lips the way a dog does before pouncing as soon as it spots a bone. Someone who sells his only sister for some cash – he's not a brother, he's not even a human.

A dog desperately gnawing a bone until it's dribbling blood from its own jaws and licking it up, that's what you are – now you're selling your sister.'

My brother became even more enraged. He rained down slap after slap on my cheek. I stood there, hissing like a cobra. 'Oh, being a strong man, are we? I'll call my Balesar – let's see who the bigger man is. Who becomes a strong man by slapping around a woman?' Saying this, I bolted towards the door, trying to escape, but my brother leapt on me and grabbed hold of me.

A sharp pain bloomed across Gulabiya's forehead... *Bhaiya is grabbing me by the hair and tying me up with thick rope. I struggle against him, but it's all in vain. At the end of the day, I have to admit he has a man's strength, and I cannot put up a fight.*

I think of Balesar. He will be waiting for me on our fields, but he won't be able to meet me. The evening before, I met him before making my way home. He drew me into his arms and said, 'Look, Gulabo, the happiest day of your life will be here soon. The day all the bananas of this field are sold, I will come to your house and ask your brother and sister-in-law for your hand in marriage. We will spend the rest of our lives together. Yes, that day is close now when, with these very hands of mine, I'll fill your milky-white parting with blazing red sindoor.'

Remembering this, Gulabo's hand drifted to her

parting. It was still milk-white – bare, desolate. Restlessly longing for a hand to fill it with sindoor.

Balesar was so restless and eager when he said, 'I will come to you soon.' I was so thrilled. But god has deserted us. On my way home, it's as if I toppled the wheel of fortune, and all joy and happiness have fallen away.

From that day until now, Gulabiya had known nothing but sorrow. She hadn't eaten well, hadn't slept well. Thoughts of Balesar would come to her – what must have happened to him? Had he sold the farmland or not? She was sure Bhumi Babu must have had it sold. Whether it was Bhumi Babu or Patel Singh – they were two eyes of the same monster. Surely Balesar's peace and happiness, his home and hearth, all of it had been swallowed whole.

Balesar had mortgaged his home and land to pay for the farm. He must have lost everything – the home, the banana farm. *Who knows where he stays, what he eats. He must be completely defeated and helpless without me.*

He has never eaten without me, not even for one day. Until I feed him, he won't eat. I have to cajole him into eating from my hand. A man's mind can be so womanly – I realized this after being with Balesar. Truly, a man is Ardhnarishvar – half man, half woman. Who is there to feed him now? Who asks after a man who has lost his home and land? He must be sinking into madness thinking about me. There's no one I can ask about him – not even a bird.

The more she thought about Balesar, the more she felt love wash over her, like sugar dissolving in water, salt melting away… Suddenly, it was as if Balesar was there, standing at the door, calling to her. 'Gulabo, I have come. I have not eaten without you in days. I could not eat a single morsel. Gulabo, I have come…' She couldn't tell – was this a dream? Was it real? Frantically leaping up, she ran to the door. But the room was locked. She began to beat her head against the door and scream. 'Open the door. My Balesar has come – he's at the door, calling for me. I can't live without him.'

Gulabo spent an hour beating her head against the locked door, calling Balesar's name. Just like before, a crowd gathered at the entrance, and children came, thinking it was some kind of game. Basant was in his room, hissing with rage like a snake, wanting to kill her with his venom. Basant's mother clutched her son tight, saying, 'Son, don't do this. If she dies, you'll spend the rest of your life going between courts and jails.' For the next few days, Gulabo continued to bang her head on the door, unceasing, unrelenting.

Soon, the whole village knew – Basant had driven his bride to madness. And after driving her mad, he beat her, not sparing her for a second. Gulabo was used to it by now. The people of the neighbourhood tried to reason with Basanta Mai. 'Don't let this happen, Basanta Mai – stop him from committing this cruelty. Even an executioner has more pity on living creatures than this. Now it's a question of your family's honour too. Don't do this. After all, she's a human being. This kind of rage and violence is not good.' And it wasn't just the neighbours coming to her to say this, it was everyone, young and old. In the end, Basant calmed down a little.

As Basant softened, Gulabiya grew more and more fierce. She wouldn't be quiet until a resolution was found. One evening, when Tetri's grandmother came to ask Basanta Mai for some yoghurt starter, the conversation turned to the topic of the panchayat. Basant's mother opened up the discussion, but Tetri's grandmother closed the matter.

In a clear, full-throated voice, she said, 'What is there to think about? Rather than letting this problem grow, it's better to press the wart and let the pus out. Let the panch be assembled, and whoever they decide in favour of will be the winner.'

Basant's mother responded, 'Speak softly, Maaji, that

snake hears everything – she pretends to be asleep, but she is listening.'

But Tetri's mother continued in her clear and loud tone, 'How does it matter what she hears and doesn't hear? Whatever verdict the panchayat gives, everyone will have to accept. I think the decision will be in your daughter-in-law's favour. The whole village is full of talk about how Basant beats his wife like cattle. And Basant is adding fuel to the flames, telling everyone that she has gone mad. Now tell me, why keep a madwoman in your house? I think the panch will say that Gulabo should be sent to her natal home, and then her sanity or insanity will be their problem.'

Tetri's grandmother took her yoghurt starter and left. Gulabo had been listening closely to everything, pretending to be asleep. Brightness broke out on her face, as if a ray of sunlight had cut through the fog of Magh and shone on a garden. But she concealed her feelings, and over the next few days, began to play up her madness.

The sudden change scared Basanta Mai. She hadn't been ready before, but now, she was prepared – it was time to call on the panch. If they didn't decide in her daughter-in-law's favour, she'd find a way to make them. *She has to get out of my house as soon as possible.*

A week later, the panchayat gathered beneath the

banyan tree in the western hamlet of the village. It was exactly five in the evening when the elders gathered. Even before they arrived, a large crowd had assembled. Everyone had the same questions – what decision would they deliver? Would they find in favour of Gulabiya or Basant? People gathered from every corner, the old and the young, to satisfy their curiosity.

Everyone, from Tetri's grandmother to the mukhiya Shamsher Singh, was in attendance. The panch sat in the tree's shade, cross-legged on the circular platform around it.

On one side, the women sat with their long veils, holding a corner between their teeth, peeking sideways at the panch. On the other side, the men sat facing the panch directly. But in fact, every single one of them was only half-watching the panch, their thoughts planted firmly on Gulabiya.

Gulabiya sat at the front of the crowd, directly facing the panch – without a hint of hesitation. Her husband sat at a slight remove from her. Gulabiya did not seem cowed, sitting amongst her in-laws. In fact, her face was a little brighter than usual. Her eagerness to speak was visible in her expression; her eyes said that she believed victory would be hers. The panch would find in her favour. And why shouldn't they? Then, Gulabiya would be free as a bird. She would trill like a parrot and fly her cage, fly until she reached that jungle of hers, the one where her nest was. In that nest, her husband would be yearning for her. As soon as she reached the jungle, it would ring with her chirping. Picturing all of this, Gulabiya trembled with anticipation. Her reverie was broken by the panch's questions – 'Why do you behave like this? Do you accept Basant as your husband or not? If you don't, why?'

Gulabiya stood up to speak and delivered her speech in an even tone. 'Respected panch, this man sitting beside me – he may be his sister's man, but he isn't mine. He and his sister have toyed with me and ruined my life. What sin from a past life is he exacting revenge on me for? I have never accepted him as my husband, because he filled my parting with sindoor when I was unconscious. Is this marriage any kind of marriage, where one side is silent and voiceless? Respected panch, if a pinch of sindoor, placed by any man in any woman's parting, is enough to make her his lifelong slave, his wife, then you do the same. All of you, take a fistful of senoor and rub it in any woman's parting, then claim every woman in the village as your wife.'

Gulabiya's unabashed nature and unveiled words shocked the panch and dumbfounded the men in the crowd. No one could say a word except Gulabiya, who kept going. 'Listen, you are all like my fathers and grandfathers, and you are like gods on this earth, who decide between justice and injustice. If you don't deliver justice for me, if you don't stand on the side of truth, then there will be nothing left to have faith in. If you wish to know anything more, then know this: Basant can never be my husband, my man – ever. My husband is the one I've already accepted as mine in my heart, and who has accepted me as his. If true sindoor is ever to fill my parting, it will be his.'

Hearing all this, everyone put their fingers in their ears. The panch turned their faces away and said, 'This has crossed all limits. This horrid woman is speaking sinfully, and wherever such sin goes, it eats away at the home, the village. We need to contain her here. She is not mad – she is only pretending. For this wicked woman, we have made a decision. Basant, who is this woman's husband, shall take her home by any means necessary – persuasion, payment, punishment, or deception – and bring her under control. If, in bringing this woman onto the right path, her life is lost, then so be it. The panch decrees that, in keeping with the norms and codes of the village, no case shall be brought against Basant.'

The panch had made their decision. Everyone returned home, and behind them, Basant walked, gripping Gulabiya by the arm, almost dragging her. The Gulabiya who, a short while earlier, had spoken sharply and steadily before the elders, like a lawyer arguing in court, that same Gulabiya had suddenly wilted. She could not believe that the verdict had been against her. Now she'd spend her life rotting beneath the feet of this sorry excuse for a man. There was only one way left to escape: to tear at her own body with her teeth, or to throw herself into some river or pond and die.

Dragged along, Gulabiya was a goat being pulled forward by a butcher who had a rope around her neck, not wanting to follow but being forced along. There were plenty of onlookers to this sight, but no one to save her. Such treatment of a woman was nothing but an entertaining spectacle to them.

The panch's decision had shaken Gulabo to her core. From the moment they reached home that evening, a strange transformation took place in her temperament. She still didn't speak much, but she no longer acted like she was crazy. Not just her mother-in-law, but Basant too seemed happy to see the change.

Basant's mother even went to give thanks and make pledges, from the shrine of Sheetala Mai to Jakh Baba's shrine. 'O Sheetala Mai, if you rid my daughter-in-law of her madness, I will offer you a pair of pigeons. Hai Jakh

Baba, if you fix her, I will sacrifice a pair of goats to you.' There was hardly a god before whom Basant's mother did not kneel and give a vow.

Whether it was the power of the gods or something else, a change began to come over Gulabo. Seeing this, one day, her mother-in-law came close to her and said, 'Child, what has happened has happened. When a mountain comes in the way of your life, you cannot climb it if you become withdrawn. No one can. When I was married and came here, there was a lot going on in my mind too. It's true, I didn't want to come to this house, but when I was tied here by marriage, I decided to accept the man of this house as my husband and live my life accordingly. What you see today is the result of that commitment – a full, thriving household.

'What is left in my life now? I had two daughters – both are married and settled in their own homes. This house has just one son – Basant. He must take the family line forward. And how can the family line continue without you?'

11

The entire village was abuzz with the news that Basant's mother had emerged triumphant. She was about to be a grandmother. The elders of the village couldn't stop talking about it.

Basant's mother seemed to have grown wings. New blood flowed into her ageing flesh. Her energy would put a young girl to shame.

'So, is there going to be a feast or not, Basanta Mai? I'm sure you're going to feed everyone till they're stuffed to the gills. I hear the sun is about to descend into your backyard!'

'Of course, no two ways about it! A feast to end all feasts!'

It really was very strange that Gulabiya, who had been silent, had started to engage in conversation. Not just with the people of the house, but also with passers-by on the streets. Basanta Mai felt as if good fortune was rushing back towards her.

But the other women of the village noticed something strange in Gulabiya's demeanour. Whenever the child was mentioned to Gulabiya, she appeared neither happy nor sad. Her face was inscrutable, with no feelings visible on the surface.

The women reasoned that Gulabiya, who had taken so long to conceive, was being cautious of the evil eye, and that's why she didn't want to talk about the baby.

Time flew by. Three months, four months, five, six, seven, eight, and then the ninth month was close to being over. Basant's joy was boundless.

The whole family was fussing over decorating the house to welcome the newborn, but Gulabo was at a distance from everything; she was somewhere else. She was some place where she didn't even know that she was Gulabiya. She was going to be a mother, but her heart had not a shred of maternal affection.

This sometimes worried Basant.

It wasn't that Gulabo didn't talk to him. They talked, joked, and flirted. But whenever he spoke about them becoming parents, she drifted away from him to a place where his voice didn't seem to reach her.

12

And then finally the day came when Basant became the father of a son.

Basanta Mai's household swelled with songs of joy. Jhunki Mai played the dhol, and Madhuriya Mai sang, her voice dripping with honey.

Dhanya dhanya raaj Ajodhya ki, dhanya Raja Dashrath hai
Lalna re, dhanya re Kaushalya ji ke bhaag ki Ram ji janam lel hai
Aela je pandit purohit baithla palang chadhi hai
Lalna re, guni diyo nunua ke din koun tithi janamal hai

Blessed, blessed is the land of Ayodhya, blessed is King Dashrath
Sweet boy, blessed is Kauṣhalya's fortune that Ram is born
Pandits and saints surround the cot
Sweet boy, tell them of the hour of your coming

Before this song was over, Surekha Mai had already begun singing another:

Navami tithi nunua janam lel Chait maas beete hai
Lalna re, barahe baras jab hoyte vanih chali jayat hai
Etna vachan jab sunlin aho Raja Dashrath hai
Lalna re, dharti khasal muruchai ki ab kena jeevit hai
Soyeri se bolali Kaushalya Rani, sunu Raja Dashrath hai
Lalna re, kahaun jeye mora beta baanjhi pan chhootal hai

When spring blooms in Chait, born is a babe on the ninth day
Dearest o dearest, in your twelfth year, to the forest you'll go away
Hearing this, King Dashrath weeps in dismay
Oh beloved, the earth wilts and withers, what remains to live for today?
From her bed we hear Kaushalya say
'Sweet boy, why would you leave after driving my barrenness away?'

'Oh, Basanta Mai, are you sending us off with just a plateful of songs, or do you have something else planned?'

'What else? What else would you all like? Should Basanta sell off the house and land and shower you all with gold and jewels?'

'Aha, Mai! When did I say anything like that? If you're going to do their jobs, what will the performers do when they get here?'

That day was full of jokes and laughter.

13

But now it is becoming obvious to everyone – Gulabo is not happy. Why is Gulabo not happy with her rose-like newborn?

This indifference isn't even normal for a woman to have towards another's child, but to be this detached from your own? The fruit of her own womb!

How? Why? What was the matter?

Madhuriya Mai couldn't restrain her curiosity. She had to find out the reason behind this.

She thought about all the possibilities. The child looked exactly like Basant – he was obviously the father. When there was no doubt about that, why was Gulabo acting like this?

Madhuriya Mai had to know. She couldn't help it. One day, she sat with Gulabo, talking for a long while, until she finally asked her, 'Hey, Daughter, tell me one thing –

after you've become a mother, you don't seem very maternal towards your child. Why is that?'

Gulabo listened to her query with great concern at first, and then she burst out laughing and said, 'Kaki, what maternal love? What joy? Why? Who is supposed to be overjoyed by a good crop? The field or the farmer who owns it?'

What Gulabo then went on to say so shocked Madhuriya Mai that she felt a shiver go down her spine.

'What is this, Daughter? Who told you something so vile? Don't ever let such filth fill your mouth ever again!'

Madhuriya Mai's shocked state made Gulabiya laugh even harder. She stifled her giggles and said, 'You may not believe it, Kaki, but it's absolutely true.'

'Even if this perverted business happens, why do you need to go around telling people about it? Whoever does this can do what they want. Just forget it!'

The conversation ended there.

14

Madhuriya Mai couldn't keep things to herself for long. Finally, she unravelled and recounted the whole conversation to her husband. 'Listen, let me tell you what Basanta's wife told me. She said that in big cities, women rent out their wombs. They take thirty thousand, fifty thousand lakhs, to stay with a man. Once his child is born, they leave that man and go home to their husbands.' She stopped. 'You tell me, could something like this really be true?'

'When even gods are unaware of a woman's true nature, then how should I know?' He tried to get her off his back.

But Madhuriya Mai is not done yet. 'That's not all. You know what she said? She said, "Well, I've carried this child for this man. What do I have to do with this child? Let his father deal with it. My husband lives somewhere else; he went to work. I knew he'd be back in ten months.

Now, where would I have gone for ten months? I had to keep my belly fed. So, I started carrying Basant's baby in my belly. What else was there to do? Very soon, I'll reunite with my own husband. Wherever he asks me to, I'll stay. After all, he is my husband."'

Having recounted this, Madhuriya falls into a stone-like trance for a few moments, grappling with what Gulabo had told her. Then, coming to, she asks, 'What do you think? Is she really going to run away?'

'No, no. Where does this happen? No matter how close a woman is to a man in her unmarried days, marriage changes things for good. Her husband becomes god for her. Whatever Basanta's wife told you, don't repeat a word to anyone.'

Madhuriya Mai doesn't tell anyone what Gulabiya said. Ten days later, the village will see mayhem of a kind they never have before.

—

One hour, two hours. What has happened? Gulabiya hasn't returned; she said she was just going to the outhouse. Did a snake bite her in the dark? Basant's heart pounds with fear. He goes to his mother.

His mother hurries out into the night in search of her daughter-in-law. 'Oh, Ma, I already looked outside, I couldn't find her anywhere.' Basanta Mai searches through the trees; she overturns every single leaf. She comes home, exhausted and empty-handed.

The air in the house is still, silent. But soon, the bubble is burst – how long can something like this remain private? The villagers begin to gather; the men stand apart, muttering in low voices amongst themselves.

A crowd of a hundred, hundred and fifty women in the yard. On every face, the same question – *what has happened to Basant's bride? Where could she go?*

Then, Madhuriya Mai stands up and addresses Basanta Mai, assuming the role of a mukhiya delivering a panch's verdict. 'Listen, Basanta Mai, you must let her go. She is not your daughter-in-law, nor is she Basanta's wife. She is someone else's woman; she has gone to him now. Asking after her will only spread your dishonour further. The best thing to do now is to find another bride for Basant, to bring up his child.'

Basant and his mother sit there, unable to speak – locks clamped on their mouths. The other women slip off into the night, whispering amongst themselves.

Author's Note

On the publication of the first edition

Gulabiya's serialized publication began in the Bhagalpur publication *Nai Baat*. There were a few instalments of the story remaining, but due to me being otherwise occupied, those portions did not go into print.

Unfortunately, I became so busy with life – a job as a PhD scholar, and the running from pillar to post that accompanies this undertaking – that I was unable to give the publication of the final parts of *Gulabiya* attention.

However, it so happened that Akashvani Bhagalpur aired a radio play named *Gulabiya*. This broadcast made my mind return once more to this story.

And so it is that *Gulabiya* has now come to be published. How has this book turned out? I await your responses.

January 2008

On the publication of the second edition

What can I say about the publication of the second edition of *Gulabiya*? When I was first binding the story of Gulabiya into a book, I did not know that this would one day become a radio play on Akashvani Bhagalpur. After that, *Gulabiya*'s popularity grew further. This novel has remained at the centre of women's discourse. All these things encouraged me to get a second edition of *Gulabiya* published; in fact, I myself only have one or two copies of the original print. When someone I know asks for a copy, I cannot give them one. This will no longer be a problem. To tell the truth, I am overjoyed at the publication of this second edition of *Gulabiya*. Maybe there will even be a Hindi publication some day.

May 2023

On the publication of the English translation

I don't quite remember the year, but I'm talking about three-and-a-half decades ago, when a little girl had come into my arms. My one-and-a-half-year-old daughter. Though I lived in Bhagalpur with my mother, in her house, I often visited my in-laws. My marital home is in Semapur, a well-known village in the Kosi region. This area is important from both a natural and economic point of view. The Kosi River flows from the Himalayas, bringing with it boundless water, washing everything away. It leaves behind new soil in the fields to give birth to new crops. Labourers return to their work, and the fields are once again filled with song. This region is particularly renowned for its banana cultivation.

It was in this region that I first saw Gulabiya – she wasn't older than fourteen or fifteen. So lively – she was always hopping and chirping like some mountain bird. While I stayed in Semapur, most of her day would be spent with me, because she was the one who handled my household work.

One day, I sat her down to find out what the secret was behind her happiness, what allowed her to never be sad. In response, she first simply smiled. But, just as a mountain river has no firm banks, and flows wherever it finds a path, she began speaking, 'Maalkin, the one who works with me in your fields – he really cares for me. He cares for me more than he does for anyone else.' Having said this, she lowered her eyes. Maybe she didn't want to say anything more. I didn't ask either.

Time went by. Not a few months, two years. I visited my in-laws' house after two years with my daughter, now three years old. But this time, I didn't see her. I asked my husband if she had stopped working there. By *her*, I mean the girl who used to work on my fields and in my house, who became the Gulabiya of my book *Gulabiya*.

I didn't get a straightforward reply to my question from my husband. Instead, he smiled and said, 'What of girls who work in the fields? You never know when they'll choose someone and run away.' But I was not satisfied with this answer. When I asked my sister-in-law, she told me that Gulabiya had been forcibly married to another labourer. But she didn't remain with him for more than two months. In the middle of the night, she came back to this village and left with her lover, never to return. In the beginning, they did search for her – not just her in-laws, but her parental family, too. But in the end, everyone went quiet.

When I asked after Gulabiya more widely, I found out that her husband had treated her in the worst ways a man can treat a woman – not just physically, but also emotionally. How long could the poor girl bear it? She left her in-laws and her parental home too, and ran somewhere far away.

Though she had run away, she never left my mind. I kept thinking about her. Even when I returned to Bhagalpur, I could not free myself from thoughts of her. What was new then was that when I thought of her, I would end up thinking of the state of women in our society in general. Gulabiya's plight came to seem like the plight of a large section of women. I began to turn over and examine my own life. In many ways, my life was like this, too. Gulabiya was illiterate – a simple village girl who flowed like the Kosi River. She had no awareness of where one should flow or how. For this reason, she made up her mind and chose her own path. Women from educated sections of society cannot do this – they are scared by the restraints and restrictions of society. This is the very reason many of my own desires suffocated and died. I began to think that if, like Gulabiya, I had taken steps at the right time, I might have been able to fulfil dreams that would have been instrumental to my future. But my upbringing prevented me from going against the wishes of my family.

Those days, Gulabiya and I were face to face, we'd

sleep and wake at the same time, and talk – talk beyond social limits. It is these conversations that I have preserved in *Gulabiya*. That village girl's name wasn't even Gulabiya; it is a name I have given her.

But it isn't as if that's all that is behind the genesis of this novel. After the 1960s and 1970s, many Hindi novels on the suffering of women were published. Society was progressing, and women were doing things that could not have been imagined before. It is different for such things to be in stories and folktales, but these ideas began appearing in newspapers. There were reports about women renting out their wombs as surrogates. At first, I was shocked, but then I thought to myself – what is there to be shocked about? This must have happened amongst royal families and in palaces, too. After all, what were harems made for? Thinking about all these things, I made some changes to Gulabiya's character. In the story, she becomes a mother while living in her in-laws' house and then leaves this child behind when she runs away with her lover to a distant land to live out her dreams.

This is the full background to my short novel.

December 2025

Translator's Note

Shivangi
February 2026

I found *Gulabiya* six months before my twenty-fourth birthday and I am writing this note six months away from my twenty-seventh birthday. I have since changed four houses, three jobs, and two cities. Abha ji took a lot longer to write the novel. I think she began work in 2001 and got done in 2008. I may be misremembering, though, because (as my editor will confirm) I'm horrible with dates and deadlines.

This novelette is only eighty or so pages long. What made it such a daunting task?

Angika was first identified by linguist and British civil servant George Grierson in the early 1900s, as the Chika Chikki dialect of Maithili. It was around the 1950s that Rahul Sankrityayan coined and popularized the term

'Angika'. Only in the 1970s did Angika gain sustained attention, when a movement to make Maithili the medium of instruction in schools (rather than Hindi) grew in strength. Interestingly, Angika intellectuals and language activists supported the use of Hindi over Maithili, fearing that the use of Maithili would further obfuscate Angika. Demands for a separate language status still haven't been met.

It is no wonder, then, that the print circulation in Angika is small. So, imagine my surprise when I came across *Gulabiya*. It had two editions completely sold out and a ruckus raised over its inclusion in the Angika syllabus at Bhagalpur University.

With this history, I expected a thick, imposing text with raunchy and sensational themes. Instead, I found a story that was brief, intentional, dramatic, and yet restrained.

I suppose this is true of the subject matter of the book as well. Many girls elope for love across the country. The reactions they face are often quite loud, yet the elopement itself isn't. It happens quietly in the dead of the night.

Abha Purbey's talent as a writer lies in the acute awareness of this contrast. Grand cinematic confessions of love are contrasted with long sections about the red tape involved in acquiring a loan from a bank. At no point in the novel is the reality of class or caste ever forgotten to make way for a clean romance. The book remembers where it's set. Gulabiya wouldn't actually have spoken Hindi and so her story isn't told in Hindi. The result is dialogue that is so authentic that at times when translating I felt like I was translating a taunt I'd hear at home. Yet the language choice was literary more than political. As Abha ji explained to me, if she wrote the dialogue in Angika and kept the narrative voice in Hindi, it would cause a dissonance within the text. Hindi's overtly polished and flat nature would be at odds with the blunt and musical Angika. The languages are too far apart to be harmonious.

My biggest task with *Gulabiya* was something that is any translator's primary task – letting go of the original. Two years in, I still haven't quite succeeded.

The book was too close to home. And so having a co-translator who wasn't Bihari helped. We discarded many of the extremely literal translations from our first draft in favour of phrasing that made more sense in English. In the process, my language politics also evolved.

My only rigid position with this book was to use 'senoor', meaning vermilion, instead of 'sindoor' wherever needed. It was a decision I made to 'correct' what I assumed was an editorial oversight in the original, which alternates between 'sindoor' and 'senoor'.

Arguing with Tejaswi over this made me see something I hadn't really thought of before. My own memory of Bihari languages and how they're actually spoken has now been so aggressively edited to be 'free' of Hindi, to be more 'deserving' of a language status, that I flatten the registers when I recall them. We ended up recreating the terminology as it stands in the original.

I was initially interested in translating two Angika novels, but neither had any contact details for the author on the website I found them. A brief search led me to Dr Amarendra, who is a senior scholar in the language and heads the Angika Sansad, an organization dedicated to creating a literary culture in Angika. When I called Dr Amarendra to enquire about the rights for *Gulabiya*, I was actually more interested in the other book, a fantasy fiction in the language, also by a woman author. Dr Amarendra, however, insisted that I work with *Gulabiya*. 'The first book out of Angika must be *Gulabiya*. It is what makes Angika literature distinct from Maithili,' he said. After all this time, having read more in both languages, I see what he meant.

Gulabiya is a novel one cannot help but fall in love with. Its dreams are most moderate: agency, love, and owning one's labour. The central conflict in the romance isn't internal. At no point does either party entertain the thought of letting go of each other to please societal forces. The choice for them is always each other – and they look to shape the world to meet them. When they cannot do that, they look for a world that has place for both of them. It's an Angika novel. It could not have existed in any other language.

The novel's plot seems to almost benefit from the lack of editorial structures in the Angika publishing industry. It's a woman and the page and the way she sees the world untouched, unedited.

I could write about this book all day, but the sun is setting and who has ever had the whole day?

Translator's Note

Tejaswi Rawal
February 2026

The most challenging aspect of *Gulabiya* is also its most pleasurable. This slim novel is a trickier thing than it first appears. Ultimately, it has a simple narrative, with its two central characters – Balesar and his Gulabiya – living and loving on the page. But in the telling of this story, Dr Purbey's narrator slips in and out of the characters' consciousnesses and straddles time. It can seem challenging at first to get to grips with the story, but soon, the dreamlike ambiguity takes over, and you are under a spell, suspended in the fragrant air of a banana field.

When the novel opens on Gulabiya, tilling the soil under the hot sun, we seem to encounter her through a straightforward omniscient narrator. Quite soon, we discover that something more interesting, fluid, and free is going on. The narrator of this story has the freedom to move. Though we begin at a distance, we will soon be very close to Gulabiya – the beating heart of this story.

As psychic distance gets closer, the narrator feels no compunction about dipping directly into a character's thoughts or creating ambiguity about whose head we are in. The narration slips from omniscience to particular points of view, inhabits the heads of not just Gulabiya and Balesar, but also the minor characters who surround them. The shifts and slips take place between scenes and even between sentences in the same paragraph.

In the first chapter, Paro, Gulabiya's friend, contends with a lovestruck Gulabiya, who refuses to leave the field until Balesar comes to meet her as promised.

> She is angry with Gulabiya now. What has happened to this girl? She looks at her, sitting there with a shovel in her hand. So lost in thought that she doesn't realize that her saree is beginning to slip off. Her hair is dishevelled from working. Seeing her in this state deflates Paro.
>
> She thinks of what Somen said: 'Your friend is really beautiful. She'd catch anyone's eye.' Her gaze falls on Gulabiya, like a chakor looks at the moon. But would the chakor have looked at the moon if it had seen Gulabiya first? Paro looks at her intently. Gulabiya does look especially beautiful today, truly striking, in her pink saree and blue blouse. It seems she came to work dressed up to meet someone.

Deftly done as it is, in its dreamlike present tense and lilting allusion, it's easy to miss that there's a multiplicity and ambiguity here. Who is saying, 'What has happened to this girl?' Is it the narrator or the narrator relaying Paro's thoughts? Similarly, Paro seems to respond within her thoughts to the narrator's comparison of her to a chakor.

The novel brims with this kind of image, surrounding us in the natural world of the characters. It is almost too tempting to draw on the beauty of these images; I limit myself here to three. We might slip from one character's head to another's, or perhaps to an observation about life from the narrator, with the ease of the flowing Kosi River. Or we might pause a while and listen to a particular character's thoughts, unhurried as a clear spring sky. In a moment of heightened tension, a voice may burst forth like a banana bloom.

With the banana harvest so central to the lives of our protagonists, the narrator is, of course, attentive to the seasons. Even as we mark time by the seasons though, tense shifts freely, and characters speak to each other in a kind of 'sometime'. We might ask, when are we? *Gulabiya* responds, does it matter? It happened. It's happening still.

Working on this book, I made the journey from meeting this narrator who plays with time as a challenge to enjoying the experience of swaying and singing on the way, even as tragedy unfolds and disaster strikes for the characters. In her 2019 Nobel Prize lecture, Olga Tokarczuk spoke of her dream of a 'fourth person' narrator, one who:

> is not merely a grammatical construct of course, but who manages to encompass the perspective of each of the characters, as well as having the capacity to step beyond the horizon of each of them, who sees more and has a wider view, and who is able to ignore time.

Gulabiya approaches this 'fourth person' point of view. The narrator – omniscient and yet slipping in asides of personal wisdom, occupying a seemingly multiple position in time, accessing the innermost thoughts of each character at will – invites us into the world of Balesar and Gulabiya. The narrative's playfulness gives us a moving stream, floating in which we can carve our way through the misfortunes that befall our couple, and see beyond the horizon.

I hope you have enjoyed our attempt to bring to English the simple brilliance and idiosyncrasies of Dr Abha Purbey's Angika tale. I hope you have enjoyed weaving, flowing, and flitting with the narrator through time, from a sweltering summer under the harsh sun to a quiet night thick with possibility.

About the Author

Photo credit: Sunil Kumar, 2006

Abha Purbey is a scholar and linguistic activist. She works primarily in Angika and Hindi and teaches Hindi at S.M. College, Bhagalpur. She is an active member of Angika Sansad, an independent publishing house dedicated to promulgating the cause of official recognition for Angika as a language in its own right. She has been creatively active since the early 1990s.

About the Translators

Photo credit: Aratrika Sengupta, 2025

Shivangi is a literary translator working between English, Hindi, Bhojpuri, Odia, Magahi and Angika. She is invested in the politics of language, intimacy, and vernacular memory, with a focus on uncovering lost and underrepresented narratives of women.

Photo credit: Lisa Murphy, 2026

Tejaswi Rawal is a literary translator and writer from Delhi, based in London. She is interested in material culture, print history, and meeting points of the familiar and the figurative. And cake.

RAISING READERS

Books Build Bright Futures

Dear Reader,

We hope you enjoyed reading this book and we'd love your attention for one more page, to share with you what's going on with children and books.

The number of children reading in their leisure time and for fun is in rapid decline. Young people have a lot of competition for their time, and a worryingly high number have only a few or no books at home.

If this is not a crisis already, it soon will be.

Studies have shown that reading for fun is the **single biggest predictor of a child's future success** – more than family circumstance, parents' educational background or income. It improves academic results, mental health, wealth, communication skills and ambition.

Our business works committedly to create books that are well-researched, engaging, and enduring, but here are some ways we can all raise more readers:

- Reading to children for just 10 minutes a day makes a difference
- Don't give up if children aren't regular readers – it's not just about the number of books they have or read but about encouraging interest and engagement
- Encourage them to listen to audiobooks
- Support schools and other libraries
- Give books as gifts

Thank you for reading: there's a lot more information about how to encourage children to read on our website.

www.raisingreaders.in